MW00576564

Treasure in
Texas

Bob Schaller

Baker Books

A Division of Baker Book House Co
Grand Rapids, Michigan 49516

Books in the X-Country Adventure series

Message in Montana
South Dakota Treaty Search
Adventure in Wyoming
Crime in a Colorado Cave
Mystery in Massachusetts

© 2001 by Bob Schaller

Published by Baker Books
a division of Baker Book House Company
P.O. Box 6287, Grand Rapids, MI 49516-6287

Printed in the United States of America

Library of Congress Cataloging-in-Publication Data

Schaller, Bob.
   Treasure in Texas / Bob Schaller.
        p.   cm. (X-country adventures)
   Summary: During a family vacation in Texas, Adam and Ashley Arlington follow the trail of a torn piece of paper and are led to surprising discoveries concerning the 1836 siege of the Alamo.
      ISBN 0-8010-4492-8 (paper)
      1. Alamo (San Antonio, Tex.)—Siege, 1836—Juvenile fiction. 2. Texas—History—Revolution, 1835–1836—Juvenile fiction. [1. Alamo (San Antonio, Tex.)—Siege, 1836—Fiction. 2. Texas—History—Revolution, 1835–1836—Fiction. 3. Texas—Fiction. 4. Brothers and sisters—Fiction. 5. Mystery and detective stories.] I. Title

PZ7.S33366 Tr 2001
[Fic]—dc21   2001035990

For current information about all releases from Baker Book House, visit our web site:

http://www.bakerbooks.com

Contents

"The real fans of Bob Schaller's books . . . find the seamlessly written, informative mysteries riveting . . . Schaller's books deliver up a message of understanding, compassion, and tolerance, yet escape any sort of preachiness. A kind of hybrid Nancy Drew/Hardy Boys travel guide, this series is a great way to introduce older children to the history, geography, and culture of a particular area."

Larkin Vonalt,
Park County (Montanta) *Weekly*

"Each book . . . carves out state (history) in an entertaining and enlightening way, complete with maps, web sites, and additional background material. The writing is sharp, the characters likable and the history lessons unobtrusive but informative."

Spencer Rumsey,
Newsday

"Each adventure is packed with information on the places the family visits. What better way for a young reader to get a grasp of an area's geography and history?"

Lisa Carden,
Orlando *Sentinel*

"This adventure series combines mystery, geography, and history to form an intriguing book for youth."

C. J. Putnam,
Wyoming *Tribune-Eagle*

"I'm glad the back cover calls this book 'Fiction—ages 9 and up.' All the way up, adults and seniors included. . . . Schaller smoothly feeds his readers a message on tolerance, respect and patience— a good pill for all."

Don Hall,
Aberdeen *American-News*

Remembering the Alamo

"Wow! This must have been the bravest act in American history ever!" Ashley exclaimed as she read from a brochure in her hands.

"I usually caution against such grand claims, Ashley, but in this case you may be right," commented Alex Arlington as he peered over his daughter's shoulder. The pair were standing near the entrance of the Shrine at the Alamo in San Antonio, Texas. "In fact," Mr. Arlington continued, "I think Davy Crockett, James Bowie, and Colonel Travis might even be listed in the dictionary under the headings for heroism and courage. Come on; let's go see how your mother and brother are doing in the gift museum."

Ashley followed her father across the path they were on and into the on-site gift museum. It didn't take long to spot the blond mother-son duo browsing near a display of Alamo memorabilia.

When sixteen-year-old Adam spied his older sister, he motioned her to join him. "Check this out, Ash. This place has a lot of cool stuff. I even found a book I know you'll love," he reported with a grin as he guided her to a shelf filled with books about Texas and the historic Alamo.

Ashley picked up a copy of the book Adam indicated, quickly losing herself in its pages. She barely noticed when her parents walked over to see what she was looking at.

"What did you find, dear?" Anne Arlington asked her.

"Adam pointed out this book, Mom. And it's full of great information about the Alamo. Listen to some of these descriptions," she said, then turned back a couple of pages to find the portion she had begun reading.

"San Antonio and the Alamo played a critical role in the Texas Revolution," Ashley read. "In December 1835, Ben Milam led Texan and Tejano volunteers against Mexican troops quartered in the city. After five days of house-to-house fighting, they forced General Marín Perfecto de Cós and his soldiers to surrender. The victorious volunteers then occupied the Alamo—already fortified prior to the battle by Cós's men—and strengthened its defenses.

"Originally named Misión San Antonio de Valero, the Alamo had served as home to missionaries and their Indian converts since its construction in 1724. In 1793," she continued, "Spanish officials secularized San Antonio's five missions and distributed their lands to the remaining Indian residents. In the early 1800s, the Spanish military stationed a cavalry unit at the former mission. The soldiers referred to the old mission as the Alamo (the Spanish word for 'cottonwood') in honor of their hometown, Alamo de Parras, Coahuila. The Alamo was home to both Revolutionaries and Royalists during Mexico's ten-year struggle for independence.

The military—Spanish, Rebel, and then Mexican—continued to occupy the Alamo until the Texas Revolution."

"Wow," Adam responded from his position across the aisle. "So the Alamo was actually run by the Mexican troops." All the Arlingtons shared a lively interest in the past, fueled by Mrs. Arlington's career as a history professor at a college near the family's Washington, D.C., home. She had always brought history alive for her family by sharing around the dinner table little-known, amusing anecdotes from the great events of the past, and Ashley and Adam had grown up mostly on bedtime stories of history's real-life heroes, not fairy-tale knights and princesses.

Meanwhile, her husband, Alex Arlington, was a well-known and busy Washington lawyer. He balanced his wife's enthusiasm for history with his daily discussions about the current events going on in the courtrooms and political arenas around Washington and the country. Listening to their parents, Ashley and Adam began to take an interest from the time they were small in both the past and the present. They figured they must have heard hundreds of discussions by now about how the two affected each other and what could be learned today from the history all around them.

The family always visited historical sites on vacation, and they never had to look far to find something that interested them. The family foursome paused to consider the incredible courage of the Texans and Tejano soldiers.

"There's no doubt that you can sense the very independent mind-set of the state of Texas," declared Mrs. Arlington after a moment had passed.

Adam chimed in, "It's almost like Texas is, at least in a lot of ways, another country all to itself."

Just as he spoke, one of the Alamo guides walked over.

"You really do have that right, young man," said the woman, who introduced herself as Jane Jermillo. "The spirit of this state is derived from events like the Alamo. We're not into being told what to do here in Texas. And we're not into telling others what to do either. As far as the Alamo itself is concerned, it's my favorite place on this earth. If you breathe in deeply here, you can feel the heart and soul of Texas."

With a bright smile, she excused herself, explaining that she had a group of visitors to address. The Arlingtons quickly decided to tag along and followed Jane outside.

Jane vividly recounted the battle of the Alamo, speaking with such great passion that many in the audience were moved to tears.

The Arlingtons listened as Jane explained with breathtaking detail about the rise of the Alamo, and then about the defeat that would later propel the Texans to victory.

"On February 23, 1836, the arrival of General Antonio López de Santa Anna's army outside San Antonio nearly caught those at the Alamo by surprise," Jane said. "Undaunted, the Texans and Tejanos prepared to defend the Alamo together. Colonel William Barret Travis sent out couriers carrying pleas for help from Texan communities. On the eighth day of the siege, a band of 32 volunteers from Gonzales arrived, bringing the number of defenders to nearly 200. Legend holds that with the possibility of additional help fading, Colonel Travis drew a line on the ground and asked any man willing to stay and fight to step over it—all except one did."

Santa Anna, the Arlingtons learned, brought as many as 4,000 troops to the Alamo, yet he struggled against the ragtag group of 189 defenders within its walls.

"The defenders saw the Alamo as the key to the defense of Texas, and they were ready to give their lives rather than surrender to General Santa Anna," Jane said proudly. "The final assault came before daybreak on the morning of March 6, 1836, as columns of Mexican soldiers emerged from the predawn darkness and headed for the Alamo's walls. Cannon and small arms fire from inside beat back several attacks, but the Mexicans regrouped and scaled the walls to rush into the compound. Once inside, they turned captured cannon on the long barracks and the church, blasting open the barricaded doors. The desperate struggle continued until the Texan and Tejano defenders were overwhelmed. By sunrise the battle had ended, and Santa Anna entered the Alamo compound to survey the scene of his victory.

"What met his eyes was a circle of his own dead soldiers around the body of every Alamo defender—eight Mexicans had been killed for every American. Though the lives of every Texan and Tejano within its walls had been sacrificed, the Alamo had also cost Santa Anna 1,600 of his men and had wounded 500 more. It was a high price for Santa Anna to pay, and from then on 'Remember the Alamo!' was the constant battle cry of everyone who fought for Texas's independence," Jane finished.

Awed by Jane's breathtaking account, the Arlingtons surveyed the grounds around them before heading back to the museum shop so Ashley could buy the book that had sparked her interest.

"Can we come back again tomorrow?" Ashley asked her parents, knowing that the family would soon be leaving for the day. "There's too much that we haven't seen."

"And even the things we saw today I'd like to see again, if we have time," Adam agreed.

Mr. and Mrs. Arlington exchanged pleased looks. They were happy to see their kids' curiosity and eagerness to learn about the Alamo and Texas history.

"You know," Mrs. Arlington said, "I'd like to get down to the flea market today before it shuts down. But I don't see why we couldn't come back again tomorrow. We'll be around this area for a week."

"Great," Ashley responded with a grin, then she headed for the shelf of books she had been viewing. "Hey, check this out, everyone. That's the letter Colonel Travis wrote just after Santa Anna's troops arrived in San Antonio," she exclaimed, stopping at a display case just outside the shop.

Adam walked up beside his sister and began reading:

Commandancy of the Alamo
Bexar, Fby. 24th, 1836

To the People of Texas & all
Americans in the world
Fellow Citizens & Compatriots

I am besieged by a thousand or more of the Mexicans under Santa Anna. I have sustained a continual bombardment & cannonade for 24 hours & have not lost a man. The enemy has demanded a surrender at discretion, otherwise the garrison are to be put to the sword if the fort is taken. I have answered the demand with a cannon shot, and our flag still waves proudly from the walls. I shall never surrender nor retreat.

Then, I call on you in the name of Liberty, of patriotism to come to our aid with all dispatch. The enemy is receiving reinforcements daily & will no doubt increase to three or four thousand in four or five days.

If this call is neglected, I am determined to sustain myself as long as possible & die like a soldier who never forgets what is due to his own honor & that of his country.

Victory or Death
William Barret Travis
Lt. Col. Comdt.

P. S. The Lord is on our side. When the enemy appeared in sight we had not three bushels of corn. We have since found in deserted houses 80 or 90 bushels & got into the walls 20 or 30 head of Beeves.
Lieutenant Colonel William Barret Travis
February 24, 1836

"Incredible," Mr. Arlington said after hearing Colonel Travis's inspiring words. "I've never heard of an act of higher bravery."

"Me either," his wife agreed. "We should get going now, but we'll definitely be back tomorrow."

The Ancient Vendor's Story

"Turn here! There's the flea market," directed Mrs. Arlington as she looked out the window.

"Looks like we got here just in time, Mom," noted Ashley. "Some people are already packing up to go home."

The flea market was scheduled to be open for another hour, but several of the tents were coming down and tables were being folded up as vendors prepared to wrap up another weekend. The Arlingtons quickly moved out of their vehicle to browse the remaining tables. On one table the girls found several colorful knitted quilts, many of them with the familiar Texas star.

"How much for one of these?" Mrs. Arlington asked the woman behind the table as she traced the famous Texas star with her finger.

"It's the end of the day, so how about twenty dollars for one or fifty dollars for three?" the woman said.

"You've got a deal," Ashley's mother agreed. As she paid for three blankets, she asked the woman for some tips about which vendors they should be sure to check out.

"The best advice I can give you is to be careful what you buy here," the woman answered.

"Why is that?" Mrs. Arlington asked.

"Because you'll hear a lot of grand stories about the stuff people are selling, especially the older stuff," the woman answered. "Some people claim to have artifacts from a hundred years ago. But sometimes that's not really true."

"So stay away from that stuff?" Adam asked.

"In most cases, yes," the woman said. "I'm not saying there aren't some great things here. Sometimes antique collectors have picked up some real gems here. But a lot of people have been fooled into thinking they are buying something really valuable—like a stirrup from a saddle once used by Santa Anna—when there's really nothing special about the item. Bottom line is that if it seems too good to be true, then . . . "

"It probably is too good to be true," Ashley chimed in.

"You've got it," she nodded as she placed the last blanket in a bag and handed it to Mrs. Arlington.

"Thank you," said Mrs. Arlington, tucking the bag under her arm. "We'd better keep moving before everyone packs up," she reminded her family.

The foursome walked slowly around the market, seeing all kinds of trinkets and mementos. Some were incredibly detailed and were obviously made by hand. After a few minutes, the guys drifted off to the side a few tables down as Ashley and her mother surveyed some pottery.

An elderly Hispanic man caught Adam's eye as they ambled down the aisle.

"Habla español?" the man asked as the father-son duo approached him.

"Cool. Looks like I get to use some of that Spanish I've been studying so hard this year." Adam grinned at his father before introducing himself to the vendor.

"You'll have to translate for me, son. French was my strong point, not Spanish," Mr. Arlington responded.

Adam nodded, then turned his attention back to the small, slightly built vendor who had identified himself as Antonio Gregorio Esparza. The man was now speaking rapidly as he pulled a dusty holster from a pile of goods behind his table. *"Jovencito, esta pistolera puede ser suya si la quiere,"* he animatedly declared, indicating that Adam could purchase the holster if he wanted it.

The holster was worn out, the brown leather faded and chipped away for the most part. Its fasteners were long gone, though the worn holes were still very visible.

"This is an awesome souvenir, Dad!" Adam said.

Mr. Arlington looked at the holster, not daring to take it from the vendor because it was so worn it looked as though it might come apart.

Mr. Esparza again addressed Adam, telling him that the holster had been passed down to him by his father. He claimed that his father had told him that the holster was once worn by one of the defenders who battled Santa Anna at the Alamo.

Adam's eyes lit up at that bit of news.

"Remember what the blanket vendor told us, Adam," his father cautioned. "Don't you think that such a historic item would be in a museum somewhere?"

Mr. Arlington chose his next words carefully. He knew the man might be fabricating his own legend here. Yet he and Adam's mother had always taught their children not to judge others. And to call Mr. Esparza's bluff would have been disrespectful.

The man must have sensed Mr. Arlington's doubt, because he turned back to Adam and spoke again.

"Dad," Adam explained after listening to what the man had to say, "I don't think he's lying to us. He says he doesn't know how many days he has left on this earth. He's ninety years old, and this is probably his last trip up from Mexico to sell goods at the flea market here in Texas.

"He says that he just wants to sell anything that he can so he doesn't have to take it back to Mexico with him tonight. He admits that he doesn't know the exact story about the holster. But he does remember hearing his father speak about it to one of his uncles. He doesn't know a lot about it, except that his father referred to the Alamo."

Mr. Arlington still wasn't convinced, but he patiently listened as his son continued to make his case.

"Dad," Adam said, "I think Mr. Esparza feels bad that we don't believe him. He says he doesn't want to pressure us into buying the holster, because he doesn't want anyone to feel bad about something they purchase from him."

Mr. Arlington ducked his head, sorry that the man had been offended by his lack of enthusiasm. "I'm going to leave this decision up to you," he told Adam.

Adam looked at the holster in awe. It was heavy, probably weighing about ten pounds without anything in it. He looked toward the man. *"Cuanto cuesta?* How much?"

"Jovencito, se lo vendere por $50," the old man responded quickly, seeming encouraged that Adam was still interested.

Adam turned to his father. "He says he will sell it to me for fifty dollars," he told Mr. Arlington, then turned his head to hear as the old man continued to speak.

When the man finished speaking, Adam turned back to his father. "He was offered a hundred dollars by a collector earlier today, Dad. But he didn't want to sell it to someone who was only looking to make money off it."

"I think I know where this is heading, Adam," Mr. Arlington said to his son. "Are you sure about this?"

"Definitely, Dad. Can I borrow twenty dollars from you?" Adam asked. "I only have thirty dollars with me, but I'll pay you back. I promise."

Mr. Arlington was surprised by his son's passion for the holster, but he still wondered about its history.

"Well, Adam," he said, "I can tell this holster is very, very old, so maybe the story behind it is interesting. But I don't want you to be too disappointed if it's not really connected to the Alamo, okay?"

"I understand, Dad. But I still think it could be, and I wish we knew how to see if it is."

"Well, if there's a way, I'm sure you'll find it," Mr. Arlington responded with a good-natured grin as he remembered all the other family vacations his children had turned into fact-finding missions. It seemed the pair had a knack for uncovering mysteries that needed unraveling.

"I hope so," Adam nodded as he added his dad's twenty-dollar bill to his own money and paid the old man.

"*Gracias, Señor,*" Adam said with a smile.

Mr. Esparza accepted the money and reached under the table into a box to retrieve a woven sack. He indicated to

Adam that he would give him the sack as well, since it would make a nice covering for the holster.

Adam thanked him and extended his hand. Mr. Arlington followed suit.

"*Dios lo bendiga y a su hijo.* God bless you and your son," Mr. Esparza said as they shook hands.

With his newest treasure in hand, Adam and his father walked over to where Ashley and Mrs. Arlington had been shopping at another table.

"Check out what I got!" Adam proclaimed proudly.

"My goodness," his mom said. "A holster. And an old one at that."

"Yep," Adam answered. "Isn't it cool?"

"Adam will be doing some extra chores when he gets home," his dad added. "He's twenty bucks in the hole, so I think he'll be taking out the garbage and washing both of our cars for the next month."

"Still a bargain, Dad, no matter how you slice it," Adam answered, his grin indicating that the extra work would be well worth the investment.

"There must be a story behind this holster," Mrs. Arlington commented, noting the teasing glances being exchanged by her husband and son.

Adam looked at his father. "Like you wouldn't believe, Mom," he responded.

"It kind of looks like it's going to break," Ashley said.

"I know," Adam said. "I'll have to take good care of it. But it's worth it to have what could be a real piece of history. I'll tell you all about it later."

History in a Holster

San Antonio was beyond picturesque to the Arlingtons. The incredible Riverwalk defied description.

In fact, the whole trip had been pretty incredible. When business called Mr. Arlington to Colorado for a special conference, the family decided to tag along and tack on a trip through Texas on the way home.

It had taken the Arlingtons two days to drive across Texas, passing countless miles of prairie and railroad tracks along the way. For Adam and Ashley, who were used to the crowded Washington, D.C., terrain, the vast Texas landscape was impressive.

The family had arrived in San Antonio tired, but the trip to the Alamo and flea market had energized them and motivated them to learn more. They wanted to see as many sights as possible while they were in town. On their way to the Rivercenter Hotel where they had reservations for the night, they began making plans for the coming days.

Upon arriving at the hotel, they decided to unwind for a while, taking some time to go through their purchases and prepare for the next day's activities.

"I have an idea," Mrs. Arlington suggested about an hour later. "How about we head down to the boats and hear more about San Antonio by riding down the river?"

"You know what, Mom?" Ashley responded, after a quick glance at her brother. "Why don't you and Dad go together—have some quiet time for just the two of you? There are a whole bunch of restaurants along the Riverwalk. You and Dad can just have a night out."

Mr. Arlington smiled widely at his wife. "Our daughter," he said, "is thinking exactly what I was thinking."

Mrs. Arlington returned her husband's smile, then turned to Adam, who was deep in thought, staring at his holster.

"Adam," she said, "what do you think about that?"

Adam set down the holster. "I think it really does have some history in it, Mom, but I don't have any facts to back it up," Adam admitted.

Mrs. Arlington chuckled at her son's oblivion to the conversation around him. "That's great, honey," she encouraged him, "but we were talking about your father and I going out alone tonight. Are you all right with that?"

Ashley laughed. Adam blushed.

"Oh, sure, Mom," Adam said. "I want to check the Alamo's web site anyway. That'll keep me busy for hours."

Adam Arlington kept busy with a lot of things. Besides his natural talent for Spanish and his other school studies, he kept up a good-natured athletic competition with his seventeen-year-old sister. They were both active in sports, but Adam took the honors on the cross-country team at Thomas Jefferson High School, while Ashley kept busy as a starter on both the TJHS basketball and volleyball teams.

The kids both had blond hair like their mother and also had her lean, athletic frame. Mrs. Arlington was an avid runner and kept the whole family in shape by suggesting challenging physical activities, especially on vacation. They had gone biking, hiking, spelunking, and mountain climbing on other vacations, to name a few.

Adam had one special area of interest, however, that no one else in the family could keep up with—he was a computer whiz, and he could make, find, or do just about anything on his computer or on the Internet. He often used his laptop to enhance the family's vacations by finding maps, places to visit, and special information for them as they traveled. That's what he planned to do with his time tonight while his parents went out for their time alone.

Mrs. Arlington was pleased by her son's eagerness to learn and grateful her children understood that their parents needed quality time alone.

Mr. Arlington glanced at his watch. "It's about 6:30 right now. We could get going and catch a boat ride for a while, then hop off on the way back at whatever restaurant sounds good," he suggested.

"Sounds great to me," his wife responded. Picking up a light jacket, she also handed her husband a pullover.

"We won't wait up for you," Ashley teased.

"It won't be too late," Mrs. Arlington replied.

Ashley and Adam stood as their parents headed to the door, then closed the door behind them.

"Want to join me for a swim?" Ashley asked her brother.

"Go ahead, sis," he answered. "Are you hungry, though? I think I'm going to get a grilled cheese downstairs and bring it back up and go online for a while. Do you want me to get something for you too?"

Ashley headed to the bathroom with her swimsuit. "I'm still full from lunch, so I think I'll work it off in the pool and then get something to eat," she answered. "Have a good time, though. I'll be down at the pool if you need me."

"Okay, Ash," Adam said, then headed downstairs. He noticed some travel brochures in the lobby while he waited for his order, so he grabbed a handful before heading back to the family's room on the twenty-third floor.

After setting up his laptop and plugging it into the phone, he logged on.

"Hmm," he murmured as he checked his e-mail. He had a few notes from friends back home. He responded with a brief message about the Alamo and—of course—the holster he had bought that day.

With that done, he went to the Alamo's web site and started scanning. When he found a section about "defenders of the Alamo," he was intrigued.

The site recounted how Davy Crockett had had a long, decorated political career in Tennessee. But after losing a congressional election in 1835, Crockett decided to head off to Texas. Adam read part of the last known letter Crockett wrote before heading to Texas.

I must say as to what I have seen of Texas it is the garden spot of the world. The best land and the best prospects for health I ever saw, and I do believe it is a fortune to any man to come here. There is a world of country here to settle.

Adam thought about the vast terrain they'd covered in the past two days and had to agree with Crockett that Texas was a "world of country." He smiled as he continued reading.

I will set out for the Rio Grande in a few days with the volunteers from the United States . . . I have but little doubt of being elected a member to form a constitution for this province. I am rejoiced at my fate. I had rather be in my present situation than to be elected to a seat in Congress for life. I am in hopes of making a fortune yet for myself and family, bad as my prospect has been.

The web site continued to talk about how Crockett was among the Tennessee Volunteers at the Alamo and about how that group had defended the most vulnerable spot at the Alamo when Santa Anna attacked.

Wanting to learn more about James Bowie, Adam poked around at other segments of the site. He admired the defenders' courage as he read about how Bowie, though clearly incapacitated by injury or illness during the battle, bravely stayed the course. Adam also read about how Bowie had lost his wife and most of her family to illness before the Alamo battle.

"Wow, that's being really tough," Adam exclaimed to himself as he continued reading about Bowie's exploits.

Bowie, Adam learned, had also been a hero in previous key battles and skirmishes in Texas, showing the valor and toughness that created the legend he remains to this day. At the Alamo, Bowie was actually rather out of the picture,

ill in a cot from what some believed was advanced tuber-
culosis. Adam read about Bowie's final moments.

On March 6 the Mexicans attacked before dawn, and all
188 defenders of the Alamo perished. Santa Anna asked
to see the corpses of Bowie, Travis, and Crockett, and
Bexar mayor Francisco Ruiz identified the bodies. Bowie
lay on his cot in a room on the south side. He had been
shot several times in the head. During his lifetime he
had been described by his old friend Caiaphas K. Ham
as "a clever, polite gentleman . . . attentive to the ladies
on all occasions . . . a true, constant, and generous friend
. . . a foe no one dared to undervalue and many feared."

Adam stared at the holster, which was over in the
recliner. He imagined that Bowie must have been, like the
others, wearing a holster similar to that one.

Turning back to his computer, Adam called up the biography of Lieutenant Colonel William Barret Travis, one of
the other defenders mentioned in the brochures he had
picked up earlier in the lobby. Travis was only twenty-six
when he was killed as the commanding officer at the Alamo.
Adam eagerly read about the former South Carolina lawyer.

Governor Henry Smith ordered Travis to recruit 100
men and reinforce Col. James C. Neill at San Antonio
in January 1836. Travis was able to recruit only 29 men.
Embarrassed, he requested to be relieved. Smith insisted
that Travis report to Neill, and within a few days Travis
found himself in command of about 50 men. Neill took
leave. When James Bowie arrived with 100 volunteers,
he and Travis quarreled over command. They were able
to effect an uneasy truce of joint command, until
Bowie's illness and injury from a fall forced him to bed.
Travis directed the preparation of the Alamo against the

arrival of Santa Anna and the Mexican army. He strengthened the walls, constructed palisades, mounted cannons, and stored provisions inside the fortress. He also wrote letters requesting reinforcements, but only the men from Gonzales came, raising the number of defenders to 189. Travis's letter addressed "To the People of Texas and All Americans in the World," written on February 24, two days after Santa Anna's advance arrived in San Antonio, brought more than enough help from the United States—but it did not arrive in time. Santa Anna ordered an assault on the Alamo just before dawn on March 6, 1836. The Mexicans overpowered the Texans within a few hours. Travis died early in the battle from a single bullet in the head. His body and those of the other defenders were burned. The nature of Travis's death elevated him from the mere commander of an obscure garrison to a genuine hero of Texas and American history.

Adam's mind was racing, but his body was ready for a break. He logged off and sat in the recliner, holding the holster across his lap. Before long he drifted off to sleep, his mind quickly drawn down the road to the Alamo.

"Come on, Private Arlington!" a sergeant called out. "It's dark out, and I see a lot of movement out there. The attack could be coming tonight!"

Adam rode his horse, brown with a white stripe down its nose, across the compound. Cannons sounded in the distance, and the second shot hit the front of the fort, knocking down part of a stone and wood barricade.

"Sir, we are fortified near the long barrack, but for how long, I do not know," Adam said to the commander.

"Private Arlington, it is victory or death!" Lieutenant Colonel Travis told him. "Go back and tell the men with you to hold their post as long as they can. I will meet the enemy head-on!"

Adam turned his horse and saw flashes from rifles and cannons in the distance. The Alamo defenders were out-numbered—maybe even 40 to 1. Adam reached for his gun but found no weapon in his holster as someone shook him by the shoulder.

"Hey, you all right, Adam?" a voice asked.

Adam opened his eyes. Ashley was waking him from his dream. His hand was deep within one of the empty pockets in the holster.

"Yeah," Adam said in a groggy tone, "I'm fine. Just napping, you know."

His sister patted him on the head.

"Looked like you were having quite a dream," she said. "You looked pretty tense. Otherwise I would have let you sleep. It's almost ten, so we should probably head to bed anyway pretty soon so we'll be ready for tomorrow."

"Hey," Adam said, pushing his fingers down in the holster as his sister spoke. "I feel something down here, some leather string or something."

Ashley came over to him and held the holster as he pushed his hand deeper.

"There's something sewn in here," Adam said. "Should I take it out?"

Ashley peered in from the best angle she could get. "You know, this holster is so brittle and old, taking out what you found inside might destroy it," Ashley said. "Maybe we can gently turn it inside out."

The pair tried, and just when it seemed they had it, the pocket on the holster split open.

"Oh no!" Adam exclaimed. "It tore!"

"We can fix it," Ashley said. "But look, what is that?"

Adam undid the rest of the lacing and pulled out a small leather bag, about two inches wide and two inches high.

"Sewn shut," Adam said. "Foiled again!"

"Do you want to open it?" Ashley asked. "I think we can do it. But this thing is yours, so if you don't want to mess with it, that's up to you."

"What would you do if it were yours?"

Ashley shrugged. "Can't make this call for you, little bro," she said. "This is your baby all the way. Mom and Dad are always talking about considering all of your options—how about that?"

"Well, we could wait for them," Adam said. "Or we could take it to a museum or somewhere."

"That's a good thought," Ashley replied. "But that would be assuming this is something that's really a big deal. It could just be a shopping list or something."

"A shopping list from a hundred years ago?" Adam asked. "Well, that would still be pretty cool! It would be like 'Hay for the horses, and nails and horseshoes from the blacksmith's shop.'"

"You know what I mean, you goof," Ashley said, laughing. "I'm just not sure it's worth taking somewhere else. If you feel like we can get it out safely together, then maybe you should do that. But if you want to wait or just forget about it, that's fine too."

Adam pursed his lips together. He knew his curiosity would get the best of him sooner or later.

"Let's see what it is," he decided.

"I was hoping you'd say that," Ashley said with a grin. "You know I can't stand an unsolved mystery."

"You and me both, Ash," Adam admitted. He went over to his suitcase and retrieved a small pocket knife, then he gently broke open the stitches. A yellow—almost brown— piece of paper slid out and quickly fell to the ground like a piece of confetti.

"Wow!" Adam said.

"Don't touch it!" Ashley said. "Flip it over gently with the knife blade or something. That thing looks so frail that it might break if we even touch it with our hands."

Adam did as his sister instructed; he gently put the blade under the paper, which was folded in half. It looked like it would be slightly more than three inches by three inches when—and if—it was finally unfolded.

"Let's be patient," Ashley reminded her brother. "We'll unfold it slowly."

Adam picked up one of the tourism pamphlets he had discovered downstairs earlier that evening and gently set the frail scrap of paper on top of it.

"Look," Adam said. "It looks like there are words inside it!"

"Gently open it, if you can," Ashley urged him.

Adam could see through the paper that there was script writing, with long strokes from ink that might have at one time been thick but had thinned with time.

"Here, I'll set it on the desk," Adam said. "You'll have to do it, Ash. My hands are shaking too badly."

Ashley smiled. "Sure thing, Adam. I wonder what you have here."

Gently Ashley opened the paper. The folds were so pronounced that she thought it would destroy the paper to flatten it. The top and bottom had been ripped off the strip of paper, so obviously it had been part of a larger piece at some point, but for whatever reason it had been torn off.

"Wow!" Adam said. "Let's turn it toward the light so we can read it."

Ashley was just as excited as her brother. The two looked at the paper carefully, and Adam read the words aloud slowly.

that was his thought. Yet if they are looking for an edge, they will miss the target. JB knew better; that is why he did it. He anticipated the attack two weeks early, even though he was ill and getting worse. But I assume they are still there. Do not fail to remember that we are the only two who have knowledge of this. This is a link to San Jacinto, to Goliad. You understand that as a Tejano, I have an obligation

"Cool!" Adam exclaimed. "This is amazing. What do you think it means, Ash?"

Ashley quickly reread the message. She tried to make sense of the words.

"Who are 'they,' I wonder?" Ashley said.

"Who or maybe 'what'?" Adam suggested.

"I'm not sure we have enough information to make sense of this," Ashley said. "Look at the edges. We're missing a good chunk of it on one or two sides. If we had either, I think we'd have a better context. Any information would help."

Adam paused for a second. Then remembering something the man at the flea market had said, he leaned forward, barely able to contain his enthusiasm. "The man who sold it to me, Ash!" he said.

"What about him?" Ashley asked, sitting back so as not to soak in all of Adam's considerable excitement.

Taking a second to gather his thoughts, Adam recounted how he and their father had approached the man.

"And that was right after we had heard about how vendors could be making outrageous claims about the history behind some of the older things at the market."

"I remember that," Ashley said. "We were told not to believe things that sounded too good to be true."

Adam nodded his head. "Yes, and I agree with that," he said. "No doubt there might be some vendors there who would promise the stars to try and make a sale. But Mr. Esparza was different; it was his first time at the market, and he lives in Mexico. Ash, this guy was ninety years old."

Ashley was still looking at the paper, trying to interpret another clue. She looked at Adam.

"What was his claim?" Ashley asked.

Adam stared at the holster. "Well, he said it had been passed down to him by his father," he said. "His father's claim was that the holster had been used at the Alamo. Of course, Dad was ready to leave right then. But even he could tell the thing was very old and had, at least at some point in time, had a lot of importance to someone. I mean, this thing is just plain old, no matter what its history is."

"And the Alamo angle—that's awesome if it's true," Ashley said.

Adam thought for a second. As things started to make sense, he jumped to his feet.

"Ashley, it *has* to be the Alamo!" Adam declared.

He paced back and forth, then stopped.

"Think about it," Adam said, pointing toward the paper. "It says 'he anticipated the attack.' And that's exactly what happened at the Alamo."

Ashley rubbed her chin. She knew her brother was still reaching a bit, but what he said certainly could make sense.

"And Goliad. That was another battle, I think," Adam said. "I kind of remember hearing or seeing something about San Jacinto too. I don't exactly remember what it was, but I think it had to do with the Alamo somehow."

Ashley grinned, impressed with how her brother had learned so much about the area's history so quickly. Her curiosity was now fully piqued, and she wanted to figure out the message on the old paper as much as Adam did.

"Answer me this one," she said. "Who is JB?"

"That could be a tough one." Adam paused. Suddenly he exclaimed, "Wait a minute! It's got to be James Bowie! He was sick at the Alamo, and this note says 'he was ill.' Ash, it has to be Bowie!"

Ashley looked up at her brother. "That actually makes sense," she said. "That's amazing! What, did you used to live at the Alamo or something?"

"Kind of," Adam said, remembering the dream he'd had after spending a couple of intense hours at the Alamo's web site earlier in the evening. "But it does make sense."

Just then the pair heard a sound at the door. Their parents came in, laughing at something they had apparently seen or heard while coming up on the elevator.

"Hi, kids!" Mr. Arlington greeted them. "I thought you two weren't going to wait up for us," he said, noting the late hour.

"Anything interesting happen while we were gone?" Mrs. Arlington asked as she removed her jacket and walked across the room to join the brother-sister team.

Adam stood and turned, wearing a look of utter disbelief at his parents' questions. He looked at Ashley, who started laughing so hard she bent over at the waist.

"Interesting?" Adam asked. "Are you kidding me?"

Mrs. Arlington walked toward the holster, noticing the piece of paper under the light.

"Looks like something might be up, Alex," she said to her husband.

"How's that?" he asked his wife. "They couldn't have covered more ground than we did tonight—we walked miles."

"Oh, Dad," Ashley said, "if you only knew!"

What's in a Name?

"If I only knew what?" Mr. Arlington asked as he hung up his pullover and his wife's jacket.

Ashley grabbed her father's arm and pulled him across the room to where her mom and Adam were standing, looking over the note.

"What is this?" asked Mrs. Arlington.

Adam glanced at his sister. "You want the long version or the short version?" he asked.

Ashley giggled.

"What do you mean?" their father asked.

"I mean we could go back to late 1836 and work our way up to today," Adam said with a smile.

"Or you could just start with tonight," Mrs. Arlington interjected.

Adam, grinning, began recounting the evening's events.

"I spent some time on the Alamo's web site and found a bunch of interesting stuff," Adam said. "When I logged off and sat down in the chair, I ended up dozing off and having a dream about the Alamo. Ashley came back to the room and found me checking out my holster in my sleep, digging my hand deep into it in search of my weapon."

He paused briefly, then continued to tell his parents how he and Ashley had found the small leather case that was stitched shut with the note inside.

"And here's what we found in the pouch," Adam said, pointing to the paper. "But be careful, this is very delicate."

The adults read the note, their eyes widening.

"This is quite something, kids," Mr. Arlington admitted. "I don't know if this piece of paper is 164 years old, but my guess is it certainly would go back to near the start of the century. So what's a Tejano?"

Adam turned on his computer. "I copied some stuff from the web site, and I saw something in there about Tejanos," he recalled. "Let me call it up real quick."

Mr. Arlington continued to survey the note.

"Here it is!" Adam said, scrolling down to a section that was titled, "How Many Tejanos Died at the Alamo?"

A number of Tejanos, or Hispanic Texans, supported the revolution and took an active part in the fight against Santa Anna's Centralist regime. San Antonio native Juan N. Seguín organized a spy company that participated in the siege and battle of Bexar. He and his company entered the Alamo on February 23. Soon after, Travis sent Captain Seguín to Goliad with a message asking for reinforcements. Seguín's men, however, remained behind as members of the Alamo garrison. Researchers have identified the following Tejano defenders: Juan Abamillo,

Juan A. Badillo, Carlos Espalier, Gregorio Esparza, Antonio Fuentes, José María Guerrero, Damacio Jimenes (Ximenes), Toribio Losoya, and Andrés Nava.

Adam turned around his seat and stood. He took two steps over to the table and peered closely at the note.

"Wait a minute!" he exclaimed. "That name from the list of Tejanos . . . Gregorio Esparza. Hey, Dad . . . "

Mr. Arlington knew what his son was thinking. "The man we met today," he remembered. "His name was Esparza, right? I didn't catch his entire name."

"Antonio Gregorio Esparza," Adam said. "That was it. I wrote it down in my wallet as we walked to the car. Wow! Could he be related to the guy who was at the Alamo?"

Ashley hadn't met Mr. Esparza but remembered seeing him. "You said he was ninety years old," she reminded Adam.

Mrs. Arlington did the math in her head. "Well, he certainly wasn't at the Alamo, because he wouldn't have been born until about 1911."

Adam looked disappointed.

"But it's possible that he could be a grandson or grand-nephew of the man from the Alamo," she continued. "Of course, there could be no link at all. Who knows?"

Adam was content just knowing there was at least a chance. "That's a good question, Mom," Adam said.

"What do you mean?" she asked.

"You said, 'Who knows?' and that's the question of the day," Adam answered. "We need to find out who knows something about this and go from there. Can we check it out back at the Alamo tomorrow?"

His parents exchanged glances. "I don't see why not," Mrs. Arlington said. "But I think either your father or I should be with you, because this note—whether it's an actual part of history or a wild goose chase—could generate some excitement and scrutiny."

"Got it, Mom," Adam agreed.

Mr. Arlington noticed how delicate the note was. "Maybe we could put this in a baggie and put it somewhere safe."

"Good idea, Dad," Adam said. "Hey, what happens in the morning? Do we take this with us?"

"That's a good question too, Adam," Mrs. Arlington said. "It would be better if we just made a copy of it."

Ashley knew that wouldn't work.

"That would break the paper; I guarantee it," Ashley said. "How about if we use that new digital camera in Adam's computer case? We could scan it in and then take it down to the office area in the hotel and print it out there. That way we can just take a couple of copies with us."

Adam's face lit up. "That's a great idea!" he said. "That way we won't damage the note."

Mr. Arlington leaned over to his wife and remarked, "Did we think that fast when we were their ages?"

She laughed and answered, "I don't think so. But you have to admit, that is an excellent idea."

Adam headed to the front of the suite, where his bed, a foldout couch, and Ashley's bed, a futon, were located. He had his computer under his arm.

"Where are you taking that, Adam?" his father asked.

Adam stopped and turned.

"Dad, there's work to do," Adam said. "I can get the picture and scan it in right now. It won't take even an hour."

"Adam, it's closing in on midnight," his mother pointed out. "I appreciate your enthusiasm. And your father and

I share your excitement. But we need to get some sleep right now. It'll still be here in the morning; I promise."

Adam had forgotten it was that late. "Okay," he said, setting down the computer. "I'm just so excited. I have a ton of ideas about how this thing could work out."

"We'll all be anxious to see what turns up tomorrow. But good night for now, kids," Mr. Arlington responded.

"Good night," Adam and Ashley chimed in unison. They talked quietly in the front of the suite after their parents closed the door to the bedroom.

"Thanks, Ash," Adam said as Ashley set up her bed.

"For what?" she asked.

Adam went over and sat down next to her.

"For helping me out earlier and for being excited about this," he said.

Ashley lightly punched her brother on the shoulder. "No problem, Adam. Anytime you find something as exciting as this puzzle, I'm behind you. Tomorrow let's print out some of the stuff you saved about the Alamo and everything relating to the heroes who were there," she said. "I want to learn more about this."

"You've got it," Adam said, heading for bed.

He thought he'd be up the entire night thinking of possible scenarios for his holster and its history. But as soon as his head hit the pillow a few minutes later, the adrenaline was gone. His body was ready to take over and get some sleep after the long day of sight-seeing—not to mention the beginning of what was possibly turning out to be a very exciting adventure.

Surprise at Goliad

The next morning after a brisk walk and a light breakfast, Adam and Ashley headed to the hotel's business center and began working on the photo of their fragile discovery. Adam carefully took a photo of the document and scanned it into his computer, then adjusted the picture to make it readable. It took several attempts to come up with a photo that scanned in perfectly and allowed for full viewing of the note, but the results were worthwhile, the kids agreed while viewing the finished product.

"We'd better hurry up and make our copies," Ashley urged her brother, while looking at her watch. "We've been here more than an hour already. Mom and Dad are probably anxious to get going."

Adam nodded in agreement and set the printer to make ten more copies.

"That should do it," he proclaimed. "Now if the folks at the Alamo want to keep one, we can leave one with them."

"Good thinking," his sister agreed as they headed back to their hotel room.

Once back in the room, the family decided to head straight out to the Alamo. They quickly walked the six blocks to the Alamo's courtyard, where they saw Jane Jermillo, the tour guide they had met the day before.

"Hello!" Jane called out to them. "It's good to see you back here today." She smiled broadly as the Arlingtons walked over to join her.

They barely exchanged hellos before an excited Adam launched into the story about the holster and their intriguing discovery.

"You've got to be kidding me!" Jane exclaimed as he handed her a copy of the note. She studied it intently for a moment, then looked up at Adam, her eyes sparkling.

"This could really be something significant, Adam," she said, shaking her head in wonder. "The note is incomplete, but what you have here does give us a few clues to go on," she noted. "The Esparza link is especially intriguing to me. That is a common name, but I'm inclined to think that there really is a good link to history here. I know of one Esparza who had some contact at Goliad. You've heard of the Goliad Massacre, right?"

"A bit," Adam answered, remembering the references he had seen on the web site the previous night. "I want to learn more, though."

"Well then, have I got a friend for you. Let me call him," Jane said. "I know he'd love to talk to you. I can't promise he'll have all the answers for you. But I think it would be worth your while to talk with him if you have the time."

Mr. and Mrs. Arlington assured Jane that the family would "make time" to do all they could to track down whatever information might be available. They explained that the family had quite a history of uncovering mysteries wherever they went, and that nothing would be able to stop their kids from pursuing this one. Jane laughed at the obvious pride in their description of the sleuthing teenagers, then excused herself to call her friend.

While Jane was busy inside the Alamo office, the Arlingtons walked around, stopping at the well that once provided water for those at the Alamo more than a century ago. They were on their way over to the long barracks when Jane came back.

"My friend, Mark Martinez, said he would be glad to see you," she told them. "Goliad's about a 112-mile drive from here. He'll meet you at the Fannin Plaza Park. I gave him your description and told him you're dripping with enthusiasm! He can fill you in on what happened there, and he says he might have another contact person for you. By the time you get there, he will have called his contact, so he may have more information for you when you arrive."

"Thank you so much," Ashley said. "We can't wait to hear what your friend has to say."

"My pleasure," Jane assured them as she shook hands with each family member. "Will you make me one promise, though?"

"Certainly," Mr. Arlington responded.

"Keep me posted, okay?" she asked. She handed the Arlingtons a card. "My home and cell phone numbers are on there. Please call me when you get back."

"We sure will. We owe you at least that much," Adam said. "We really appreciate your help."

After parting with Jane, the Arlingtons walked across the Alamo grounds and down the street back to the hotel.

"We'd better take sweatshirts or jackets," Mrs. Arlington commented, looking up at the overcast sky. "It shouldn't be too long of a road trip, but the forecast says there's a chance of rain. We'd best be prepared."

Fifteen minutes later, after a brief stop by their room, the Arlingtons climbed into their SUV and headed toward Goliad. The trip passed quickly as the kids kept up a lively discussion speculating about what Jane's friend would have to say.

"I just know this is going to turn out to be something important," Adam insisted just as his father turned off the road to park near the Fannin Plaza Park.

As the family exited their vehicle, a woman came out to meet them.

"Are you the Arlingtons?" she asked. "I'm Leslie Allen."

"That's us," Mrs. Arlington replied, extending her hand.

"Mr. Martinez had to leave, but he'll be back in about a half hour," Leslie said. "He made a few calls about your search and became very excited. He left to meet with someone a few minutes ago. He ran out of here so fast, it would have taken a horse at full gallop to keep up with him."

"Okay, we'll just wait for him to return," Mr. Arlington responded. "It's a beautiful day, so it's no bother to sit outside and enjoy it a bit."

"I do have some information about this place, if you'd like," Leslie offered.

"Oh yes, definitely," Ashley said with a smile. She took the packet of paper that Leslie handed to her. "Thanks."

"No problem. You know, this is a recorded Texas Historic Landmark," Leslie said proudly. "This city park even has a memorial column and Texas Revolution cannons. The larger of the cannons has an inscription that says, 'Used by Col. Fannin and His Men on Fannin Battlefield in Goliad County in 1836.' And they built the memorial back in 1885.

"Well, I'd best leave you folks to enjoy yourselves now," she finished.

The Arlingtons thanked her as she walked away, and Adam unpacked some bottled water while the rest of the family took seats on the grass. Ashley tore into the packet of material Leslie had given her and began to read aloud:

> The first offensive action of the Texas Revolution occurred here on October 9, 1835, when local colonists captured the fort and the town. The first Declaration of Texas Independence was signed on the altar of the presidio chapel on December 20, 1835. As 92 citizens signed the document, pledging their support to the cause of freedom, the "Bloody Arm" flag, first flag of Texas independence, was hoisted above the town.

"Wow, that sounds like some kind of flag," Adam interrupted. "Wonder what it looked like?"

Ashley shot him an impatient look. "You'd find out if you let me keep reading." She turned back to the papers in her hands and continued:

The flag was white with a sinewy red arm and hand at the center of it, grasping a drawn sword of crimson. It symbolized the Texans' willingness to make any sacrifice, no matter how great, to win their freedom from the tyranny of General Antonio Lopez de Santa Anna.

Ashley let out a low whistle. "We certainly have heard a lot about the Texans' bravery when it came to defending their freedom. No wonder they're all so proud of their history here," she commented, then she turned back to Leslie's materials.

As part of the Mexican invasion of Texas in early 1836, Santa Anna and his main force of at least 5,000 men followed an inland route toward San Antonio. At the same time, Mexican General Jose Urrea, with some 900 troops, left Matamoros and followed a coastal route into Texas. The first town Urrea approached was San Patricio, where on February 27 he encountered Frank Johnson and about 50 Texans. Johnson and 4 of his men escaped, but the rest were either killed or captured. A few days later, the Mexicans encountered James Grant and another 50 men. All but one of the Texans were killed.

Citizens of Refugio, the next town in Urrea's path, were slow to evacuate. To provide assistance, James W. Fannin, commander of the forces at Goliad, sent two relief forces. The first numbered about 30 men, the next some 150 men. Both of these groups were eventually killed or captured by the Mexicans. Meanwhile back in Goliad, Fannin and his remaining force of about 350 were called on to aid William Barrett Travis and the Alamo defenders. Afterwards, he was also ordered by Sam Houston to retreat to Victoria. Fannin failed to accomplish either of these missions. After five days' delay in following Houston's order, Fannin began his retreat. It was not long, however, before he and his men found themselves surrounded by Urrea's force on open prairie. In several attacks the Mexicans were repulsed by the deadly fire of the Texans. By dusk, the Texans had lost about 60 men killed or wounded against some 200 lost of the Mexicans.

Adam was in awe. "They never gave up," he said. "Just like the Alamo, it was victory or death."

Ashley continued to read.

Still heavily outnumbered and with no water and few supplies, the Texans waved the white flag of truce. Believing that they would be taken captive and eventually returned to their homes, the Texans surrendered the morning of March 20. They were escorted back to Goliad as prisoners. When news of their capture reached Santa Anna, however, he was furious that the Texans had not been executed on the spot, and he sent orders to now execute the Goliad prisoners.

"Yikes. Santa Anna was brutal," Ashley commented. "It says here that on Palm Sunday the prisoners were divided into three groups, marched onto open prairie, and shot. So nearly all of Fannin's men were massacred."

"That's awful!" Adam cried.

"No kidding," Ashley agreed. "But listen to what happened next." She picked up where she had left off:

The men of Goliad were martyrs to the remaining forces in Houston's army. And three weeks later the Texans sought their revenge. Inspired by cries of "Remember Goliad!" and "Remember the Alamo!", the outnumbered Texans won one of history's most decisive victories at the Battle of San Jacinto.

One of Goliad's most endearing legends was associated with the massacre here. Panchita Alvarez, wife of a high-ranking officer in the Mexican army, is credited with saving at least 28 lives by begging the commander there to spare them. Her efforts earned her the title of "Angel of Goliad."

The family took a moment to digest the thoughts.

"So this place is kind of like the Alamo, even though you don't hear as much about it in the history books," Adam observed.

"You're right, Adam. Sometimes, because so many things happen in history, textbooks have to condense things— picking and choosing certain events," Mrs. Arlington explained. "If they didn't, we history professors would have to teach around the clock to cover everything," she chuckled. "But you're certainly right about this place. It is a very special place, and some very special people— Americans, Mexicans, and Tejanos—showed a lot of courage on the very ground we're sitting on right now. There's no doubt that inspired a lot of people. And it's great to see that their spirit certainly lives on."

"What I think is cool is that Texans believe in keeping their history alive. You know, respecting the people who came before them," Adam said.

"This is definitely a cool state," his sister agreed. "Maybe I should check out some colleges while we're here. The University of Texas and the University of Houston are nearby."

"Here we go again," Adam teased. "You're never going to decide what college to go to if you keep adding possibilities to your list, Ash. Every time we go to a new state, you talk about visiting colleges."

"Your sister is just trying to keep her options open, Adam," Mr. Arlington defended his daughter. "I, for one, think that's a good idea."

"Okay, okay. I give," Adam laughed. "But right now I just want to find out more of the story behind the piece of paper we found last night."

As the family talked, two men approached them. One appeared to be in his mid-forties, while the other must have been at least seventy-five or eighty. The younger man was in a uniform similar to Leslie's, so the Arlingtons guessed that he would be Mark Martinez.

"Mr. Martinez?" Mrs. Arlington asked, standing.

"Yes, you must be the Arlingtons!" the man said excitedly. "It's great to meet you. I brought someone with me to talk with you. This is Felipe Moreno. He and I met about twenty years ago when I first got involved with Goliad."

The Arlingtons each introduced themselves and shook hands with Mr. Martinez and his friend.

"Jane Jermillo filled me in on what you've discovered," Martinez said.

Adam pulled two copies of the paper out of his folder and handed one to each of the men.

"Yes, yes," Martinez said. "Jane told me about this, and I was able to track down Mr. Moreno's number. Anyway, Mr. Moreno, I don't want to be rude and speak for you, so I'll let you handle it."

Mr. Moreno was a small, slightly built man. He appeared very genteel and spoke slowly. He told Martinez that his English was not always smooth, but he'd do his best to tell his story.

The Arlingtons smiled patiently as the old man began to speak.

"That is him, is it not?" Mr. Moreno said, a tear rolling down his cheek as he read the paper in his hand. He paused before continuing.

"My friends, do you know who gave this to you?" he asked the Arlingtons. "Was it a man named Esparza?"

Adam felt lightheaded. Ashley tugged at his arm.

"Um, yes sir, Mr. Moreno." Adam could hardly contain his excitement. "It was Mr. Antonio Gregorio Esparza. The note was in a holster that he sold me at the flea market," he continued. "He was up here just for the day. I don't even know what town he lives in—I didn't think to ask him. But he seemed to be a very kind man. Do you know him?"

Mr. Moreno pulled a red bandana from his back pocket to wipe away the tear in his eye.

"I looked for many, many years for him, but was never able to locate him," Mr. Moreno said. "I had a description of him but no location. I tried to get help from my friends in Mexico. But through the years, as all of my friends continued to move up here, I lost touch with many people I used to know. I heard about the Esparza family, but only that they had sold their farmland. I was never able to meet with Mr. Esparza or talk to him. I sent letters with his name and the towns near where I thought he might live, but they usually came back to me. And I never heard a response. I wanted very much to meet him, and I think about him every time I look at the family heirlooms in my attic."

The Arlingtons looked at each other, puzzled.

"This is the part you've been waiting for," Martinez interjected. "Mr. Moreno has a big surprise for you."

Mr. Moreno handed the copy that Adam made to Martinez. "If you would be so kind, my friend, please hold this for me," he said.

"No problem," Martinez responded.

Mr. Moreno unbuttoned his faded black leather vest, reached inside, and pulled out a large, worn brown envelope. The envelope was tied over all four sides with a piece of weathered string. He asked Martinez to hold the envelope for a moment, then buttoned his vest and put his bandana back into his back pocket.

That accomplished, Mr. Moreno extended his hands, and Martinez returned the envelope. Slowly, Mr. Moreno opened it. He pulled out a flat piece of paper that had apparently been folded years ago but was now completely straightened out.

Immediately, Adam noticed how it was torn only across the bottom. Though it was in much better condition than the piece he had found, he was screaming inside to see what it said. Being respectful of Mr. Moreno, he mustered all the patience he had and waited.

"Mr. Moreno," Martinez asked, "would you like me to read it?"

Again, Mr. Moreno's eyes were watering up. "Yes, my friend," he said, "if you wouldn't mind."

Martinez turned a bit so that the Arlingtons, along with Mr. Moreno, could look at the paper at the same time.

"I believe this is the top part of what you have," Martinez said to Adam. Then he read the piece of paper aloud:

Houston, it is of my belief that he was worried that he would be captured because of his growing incapacity, which he fought at every step just as vigorously as he fought in battle. And if captured, on the chance that he could get free, he would have access to those right away. He really thought he could take them all alone, even if he were the last man standing, did he not? So he battled to the end, and by stowing those, he could still defend the Alamo in honor, at least

"And then it picks up with our note!" Adam said. He caught himself and added, "I'm sorry, I didn't mean *our* note. This doesn't really belong to us."

"That's right, Adam. We're just caretakers of it," his mother added. "I'm sure Mr. Moreno knows you meant no disrespect to him."

Mr. Moreno nodded, appreciating the courtesy and respect the Arlingtons displayed.

"Another part of the puzzle," Mr. Arlington commented. "What do you think it means, Mr. Moreno?"

Adam was very excited. "It *is* connected to the Alamo," he whispered to Ashley. "I knew it was."

Mr. and Mrs. Arlington motioned for Adam to pay attention.

"There is a story behind this, my friends," Mr. Moreno said. "But it has all been in pieces until now. I received this paper from my uncles. I was so young when they told me, that I didn't grasp its importance at the time. But my uncle talked about the name Esparza and said that a man had passed this along to his family. Our families apparently were part of a group that found this piece of paper with a collection of mementos from the Alamo that were discovered more than a hundred years ago.

"The way the story goes, a soldier of Santa Anna's had kept a case full of things that were left behind by the Texan and Tejano soldiers who were killed defending the Alamo. He talked to a survivor—a woman, I believe—who provided care to the soldiers inside the Alamo before the final battle. She told him her story, and the Mexican soldier wrote a letter saying he could no longer support Santa Anna's brutal war tactics. He left and joined the Tejanos. He passed this letter along to a descendant of Gregorio Esparza. But from there, the trail is muddy. For instance, my family is Tejano. And while Gregorio Esparza was Tejano, the man you purchased your holster from, and his family, are Mexican, not Tejano."

"That's right," Adam said. "He said he has always lived in Mexico."

"There were many families that were split at the Alamo," Mr. Moreno said. "There were actually one or two Mexicans under Santa Anna who had Tejano brothers inside the Alamo."

Martinez asked Mr. Moreno if he could let the Arlingtons hold his piece of the note.

"Yes, of course, my friends," Mr. Moreno answered.

Adam held the note very carefully.

"I know we can't ask you for this piece," Adam said, "but I have a digital camera in my backpack. May I take a picture of your note?"

Mr. Moreno looked at Martinez as if to ask if he thought that would be okay.

Adam pulled out his camera and showed it to Martinez.

"It works with computers, Mr. Moreno," Martinez said. "I think it would be fine if Adam photographed your note, if it's all right with you."

Mr. Moreno nodded his approval, and Adam took a dozen pictures of the note, adjusting several times for lighting to make sure he had a usable picture when they returned to the hotel and downloaded it.

"I can e-mail it to you tomorrow, Mr. Moreno," Adam said.

"I'm afraid he doesn't have e-mail," Martinez said.

"But if you would like to write me letters, or get in touch with me somehow, I would be very grateful to learn whatever you discover," Mr. Moreno countered.

"I can promise you, sir, that we will do that at every turn," Mrs. Arlington said.

Martinez added, "I will be in constant contact with them, Mr. Moreno. Now that I was able to find you and I know where you live, I'll update you regularly."

Adam paused, and he sensed that Ashley was sharing the same thought.

"This still doesn't make complete sense to me. There has to be another piece somewhere," Adam determined. "What is he talking about when he says 'it was stowed'? What was stowed, and where?"

Mr. Moreno shook his head back and forth. "I cannot tell you that, because I myself do not know," he said. "I heard a story about how Sam Houston even had some involvement in this note, or at least his descendants did. But I do not really know. I am sorry, but there is nothing more I know to help you in your quest."

Mr. Moreno sighed as he finished speaking.

"I should take Mr. Moreno home," Martinez said. "This day has been taxing for him."

Mr. Moreno raised his arm. "No, no, I am very happy on this day, my friends," he said. "I am just weary."

Adam pulled out a new bottle of water, broke the seal to loosen it, and offered it to Mr. Moreno, who nodded in appreciation as he accepted it and drank from the bottle.

"The Houston thing might be an angle," Martinez said. "I can't believe all of those years, though. I mean, at least from time to time, I thought about Mr. Moreno and the time he told me about the paper. But I never really knew for sure that pieces other than his existed until today. Anyway, I think the best Houston angle might be up at San Jacinto. I don't know anyone there. But the folks who work for the Park Service up there, from what I hear, are absolutely first-rate."

With that, Martinez indicated that he would be leaving to take Mr. Moreno home. Everyone shook hands once again after Mr. Moreno had safely stowed the paper in its envelope and put it back into his vest pocket.

"We'll be in contact with you, Mr. Moreno," Mrs. Arlington said, gently patting the man on his shoulder.

"Thank you for coming into my life, my friends," Mr. Moreno said. "It's been so long, I had all but given up hope. I thank you from the bottom of my heart for giving me hope today."

Martinez wished the Arlingtons well and passed along his business card. As he walked away a few steps, he stopped and looked over his shoulder.

"Jane might know someone down at San Jacinto—or at least know someone who knows someone there," he suggested. "That might be a good option for you."

Mr. Arlington waved to Martinez. "That's a great idea. We'll hook up with her when we get back today. And we'll be in touch with you very soon; you have our word on it."

The Arlingtons were quiet as they walked back to their vehicle.

"We should probably get back to the hotel, kids. Your mom and I do have a few business commitments to take care of," Mr. Arlington said.

Ashley and Adam were disappointed.

"I wish we could head to San Jacinto right now," Adam whispered to Ashley. In the car, she pulled out the atlas.

"Look," Ashley said, pointing to where they were. "San Jacinto isn't that far from here." She tried to measure it by the scale on the map. "Maybe 230 miles," she said.

"We could be there by dark if we leave now and drive without stopping," Adam pleaded. "What do you say, Mom and Dad? Couldn't you check in with your offices from there?"

History Unfolds

Mr. and Mrs. Arlington exchanged a wary glance.

"By the time we get to San Jacinto, everything will be closed," Mrs. Arlington reasoned. "We can go tomorrow or the next day. But you two need to respect our schedules today."

As she spoke she reached for the atlas, which Ashley handed to her.

"We're southwest of San Antonio," she said, tracing the route with her finger. "And San Jacinto is northwest of San Antonio—north of Houston and west of Austin. That's a whole different trip for another day, I'm afraid."

Adam and Ashley sat back, disappointed by their mother's decision but recognizing that she was right. Mr. and Mrs. Arlington were always supportive of their kids' adventures, but they did sometimes need to keep the pair from getting carried away.

"Okay," Adam agreed, then looked at his sister as he continued. "Well, you're always saying we can view things 'as an opportunity or obligation.' So Ashley and I will go back and see Jane, and then we'll do some research on San Jacinto and learn as much as we can, so we won't have to hit the ground cold like we did today," he told his parents.

"Great idea, little bro," Ashley said with a grin. "At least we can be doing something to keep the search going."

With the siblings once again absorbed in making plans for continuing their quest, the family headed back to San Antonio, planning to get back there just after the Alamo had closed for the evening.

"Oh no," Adam sighed. "I really wanted to show this stuff to Jane. Do you think I should call her on her cell phone?" he asked.

Mrs. Arlington shook her head as she responded. "Why don't you let her digest everything we told her about today? Then we'll go by there in the morning. This is a busy time for a lot of people. We'll be able to see her tomorrow, I'm sure."

With that decision made, they turned to a discussion about their evening plans. Mr. Arlington planned to write a report on the conference he had attended in Colorado. The remaining trio decided to shop at the Rivercenter Mall and then eat at one of the restaurants on the Riverwalk.

"But first, can I at least download my pictures of Mr. Moreno's note and then print them at the hotel?" Adam asked.

"I suppose that would be okay," Mrs. Arlington agreed.

"As long as you show me how to work that thing while you're at it, that is," Ashley said, nudging her brother gently with her elbow.

"That's a deal," Adam responded.

When they got back to the hotel, Mrs. Arlington announced that she was going to take a swim before they headed out to the mall. "After all that traveling in the car today, I need to get my circulation going. Anyone want to join me?"

Adam wanted to get to work, but a little physical activity did sound pretty good after all the sitting they had done that day. "I don't really feel like swimming," he said. "But I'll ride one of those stationary bikes poolside while you swim. I'll just find some stuff on Sam Houston to read while I pedal—after I get this photo downloaded, of course," he added with a grin.

"Okay, I'll meet you down by the pool, then," his mother agreed.

"Sounds like a plan. So do you want to see how to do this, Ash?" Adam asked, holding up the camera.

"Of course," she answered, walking over to join him.

Adam talked her through the procedure as he downloaded the pictures. He had two very good images of Mr. Moreno's piece of the paper, and he couldn't decide which to print.

"That one shows the words the best—we could go with that one," Ashley said, pointing to the image she thought was best.

Adam agreed and printed it out. Again he made ten copies. Then he decided to put the two pieces of paper together on the computer. He worked for a few minutes to get them lined up just right, erasing the tear between the bottom of Mr. Moreno's piece and the top of the one they had discovered in the holster.

"Wow!" Ashley exclaimed. "Good job, little bro."

Adam was proud of his work. "Thanks," he said. "It's bizarre, isn't it? This must be how it appeared when it was first written."

All that was missing was the bottom part of the paper, the part that belonged under Adam's piece. The brother-sister team looked at each other, sharing the same thought.

"You know something, Ash?" he asked.

"I know," she said. "We might never find the other piece."

Adam sighed. "That's exactly my thought," he said. "It's almost like history is coming to life right in front of our eyes. But what happens if we don't find the other piece? We really are so close to completing this puzzle. We have two of the pieces. But the other piece could be the most important. What if we don't find it?"

Ashley shrugged. "I guess we have to do the best we can with what we have," she said. "Look at it this way, though. Just a couple of days ago we didn't have any idea what kind of exciting adventure we'd stumble across. I think we should just enjoy this ride, wherever it takes us, and wherever it ends."

"You know, you're right," Adam said. "This has already been exciting, no matter how it turns out."

"Wow, was that a compliment you just gave me?" Ashley laughed, then she punched his shoulder and went to join her mom for her swim at the pool.

Before shutting down his computer, Adam searched for information on Sam Houston. Quickly he located a short biography and printed it out. After a stop back at their room to change clothes for his workout, he scooped up Houston's biography and headed toward the workout room by the pool.

"Save that and I'll read it later, okay?" Ashley asked as Adam got settled on a stationary bike.

"Sure," he agreed, then he began pedaling and turned his attention to the papers he had printed.

Adam looked at the cover sheet about Houston, noting his nickname, "The Raven," and that he had lived from 1793 to 1863.

"Not bad for those days," Adam murmured, then continued reading:

One of the most colorful figures in Texas history, Sam Houston, was born in Virginia on March 2, 1793. He spent much of his youth in the Tennessee mountains and there became acquainted with the Cherokee Indians. He much preferred spending time with them to studies or working on the farm. With the outbreak of the second war with England, Houston enlisted as a private soldier and was made sergeant of a company. He quickly won the admiration of his men and his superiors. After receiving three near-mortal wounds at the Battle of Horseshoe Bend, he rose to the rank of first lieutenant before resigning in 1818 to study law. After a short time, he was admitted to the bar and practiced in Lebanon, Tennessee, before running for public office. He was elected to the U.S. Congress in 1823 and 1825. In 1827, Houston was elected governor of Tennessee by a large majority. Soon after, however, he quietly resigned from Tennessee politics and returned to live with his longtime friends, the Cherokees.

Adam thought about what he had just read. "What a cool guy," he said to no one in particular, "going out to live with the Indians and experiencing their lifestyle." He daydreamed for a few minutes about following Houston's example, then turned back to the biography.

He remained with the Cherokees until 1832, when he moved to Texas with a few friends. In Texas, Houston was elected delegate from Nacogdoches to the Convention of 1833, which met at San Felipe. From that time, Houston emerged as a prominent player in the affairs of Texas. He became a member of the Convention that met at Washington on the Brazos in 1836 to declare Texas's independence from Mexico. It was there that Houston was elected commander-in-chief of the armies of Texas.

Houston immediately took control of the Texas forces after the fall of the Alamo and Goliad, and conducted the retreat of the army to the site of the Battle of San Jacinto, where on April 21, 1836, his force defeated Santa Anna and secured Texas's long-sought independence. In the fall of that year, Houston was elected the first president of the Republic of Texas.

After Texas achieved statehood in 1845, Houston was elected senator from Texas to the Congress of the United States. In 1859, he was elected to serve as governor of the state of Texas. As governor, Houston was strongly opposed to the secession of Texas from the Union, and because he was much in the minority on this issue, Houston was removed from office in March of 1861, ending his illustrious career in public service. Houston retired to the privacy of his home at Huntsville, Texas, where he died in July of 1863.

Adam flipped the page to read more but found he was at the end of the biography. His appetite for information at that point was insatiable, though he did feel like he was at least a little bit versed in Houston's life and times. In fact, his head was swimming with all the information about Texas history that the family had accumulated by now.

"Too bad I'm not on 'Who Wants to Be a Millionaire?' during 'Texas history' week," he cackled. "Now that would be perfect!"

As Adam started his cooldown, a silly grin still in place, Ashley walked over from the pool.

"What's up? Looks like you're talking to the air over here," she teased.

"Oh, nothing," he answered. "Just taking it all in."

Ashley flipped her long hair over her shoulder, spraying Adam with little water droplets as she did so.

"Hey, watch it!" Adam said.

"I can see it now. You're going to be a professor of Texas history when you're done with college, aren't you?" Ashley joked.

"Something like that," Adam answered.

By the time they got back to the room and cleaned up, Adam, Ashley, and their mother decided that they were definitely hungry. But before leaving for dinner, Mrs. Arlington checked out the document Adam had constructed by merging his piece of the paper with Mr. Moreno's.

"That's good work, Adam," she said. "I know you and your sister have put a lot of time and effort into this, and what you've done—the initiative you've shown and how you've gone about it—is commendable. But just remember . . ."

"We know, we know, Mom. We might not find the other piece," Adam interrupted. "Ashley and I already talked about that."

"So what happens if you don't find it?" his mother prompted.

Adam shrugged his shoulders.

"I really don't know," Adam said. "My gut feeling is that we will. But I know we're talking about something that is really old, and we're actually pretty lucky to have come this far." He paused for a moment. "We have met some great people, at least," he commented. "Jane, Mr. Martinez, Mr. Moreno—they've all been great. And we've had a lot of fun. I guess if we don't solve it, we could turn it over to Jane or something and see what she could do with it. I'm sure she'd keep in touch with us and let us know if anything comes of it," he offered hopefully.

"I'm sure you're right. That's a great attitude," Mrs. Arlington encouraged her son. "Now, I'm starving! Let's get some food."

Quickly the three Arlingtons headed out to a place on the Riverwalk for dinner, then stopped at the mall. They did more looking than shopping, but Adam did find another book about the Alamo.

Despite his plan to start reading it yet that night, when they returned to their hotel room past 10 P.M., he decided to call it a night.

"I can't wait to get to San Jacinto," Adam said to his sister as they talked before they fell asleep.

"Me either," Ashley agreed. "I can't believe how this thing is unfolding. I can't wait to see what happens tomorrow!"

The Houston Hint

The next morning, Mr. Arlington wanted to go for a walk. Adam and Ashley couldn't wait to get going to San Jacinto. Mrs. Arlington acted as an arbitrator for the kids.

"They did relent yesterday," she said to her husband. "And we probably should get going."

Mr. Arlington sighed and decided that probably would be best.

"But let's go by and see Jane first," Ashley said.

The family walked down to the Alamo. They found Jane inside the gift shop, where she was talking to an elderly couple.

Jane saw them coming and excused herself from the couple to speak to the Arlingtons.

"I heard what happened yesterday!" Jane said. "Mark called me right after you all left Goliad. How exciting!"

Adam pulled out a piece of paper.

"This one is yours," Adam said, handing it to her.

"Amazing!" Jane proclaimed. She read the message aloud.

Houston, it is of my belief that he was worried that he would be captured because of his growing incapacity, which he fought at every step just as vigorously as he fought in battle. And if captured, on the chance that he could get free, he would have access to those right away. He really thought he could take them all alone, even if he were the last man standing, did he not? So he battled to the end, and by stowing those, he could still defend the Alamo in honor, at least

that was his thought. Yet if they are looking for an edge, they will miss the target. JB knew better; that is why he did it. He anticipated the attack two weeks early, even though he was ill and getting worse. But I assume they are still there. Do not fail to remember that we are the only two who have knowledge of this. This is a link to San Jacinto, to Goliad. You understand that as a Tejano, I have an obligation

"There's no doubt now!" Jane said. "It's got to be James Bowie—he was hurt and he was here, probably not far from where we're standing. There's little doubt he was standing in our very footsteps back in 1836. This is very likely part of the Alamo's history. But access to what? And where? We're still at least one piece short of having any sort of resolution."

Jane glanced again at the paper.

"The part about, 'if they're looking for an edge, they'll miss the target' still doesn't make sense," Jane said. "My first thought is that this might have something to do with one of Bowie's knives—for which he was so famous. But that part about missing the target tells me it could be something else. What do you all think?"

Mr. and Mrs. Arlington looked at their kids.

"These two are the ones who got us this far," Mrs. Arlington said. "So I think they'd have a better answer than Alex or I."

Adam held up the paper, and Ashley looked over his shoulder at it.

"By the line 'stowing those' I think the writer of this is referring to a weapon—a cannon or some cannonballs maybe," Adam said. "I don't know. I do know we're still missing a big part of the puzzle."

Jane nodded in agreement. "So what's the next step?" she asked.

Adam glanced at Ashley, trying to gauge her thoughts.

"We know this could be an important piece of Texas history," Ashley said. "We also know that we are basically just guests here, Ms. Jermillo. We were planning to head to San Jacinto today to see what we could find out there.

But it's your call all the way. If you want to take this over, we certainly respect that."

Jane smiled at Mr. and Mrs. Arlington.

"These are two very special young people you have," she said. "My first inclination is to take it over. But you two kids have done so well to this point. I do have several ideas. For one, we could get the media involved. That would get the word out."

"That would probably get us some good leads," Adam said. "That would get the word out to a lot more people than we could ever reach—since we're basically just driving from city to city looking for clues."

"The thing is, it could also bring people out of the woodwork and produce a bunch of wild goose chases," Jane said. "Plus, there could be some people who want to come crashing in and take it over. There could be some battles over propriety, which would only slow down the process. There could be groups with differing agendas, and who knows where that would end? So I think, if it's all right with your parents, that you two should do the best you can for now. How much longer are you in town?"

"We leave in three days," Mr. Arlington responded. "So one way or another, our end of it will be wrapping up very soon."

"Well, how about you see how far you can take this thing?" Jane asked. "And then, if you don't have closure, I would be honored to take it on and see what I can find. Really, though, the work you've done so far is amazing."

While Ashley and Adam were proud of their search so far, they also knew they hadn't gotten that far on their own.

"Ms. Jermillo," Ashley said, "we wouldn't have anything but the first piece of paper if you hadn't put us in touch with Mr. Martinez. And he did an awesome job connecting us with Mr. Moreno."

"We've just got one problem now," Ashley continued. "We know what we're looking for at San Jacinto, but we don't know where to start. Do you have any ideas, Ms. Jermillo?"

Jane tilted her head and thought for a moment.

"Actually, I don't have any contacts down there," she said. "But we do have an employee here who used to work there. She's in the gift shop right now. Let me go ask her."

Jane found Carolyn Carmen, who had moved to San Antonio from San Jacinto a year earlier. Jane introduced her to the Arlingtons and quickly brought her up to speed on what had transpired from Adam finding the first part of the note to the events the previous day at Goliad.

"This is fascinating," Carolyn said. "I only worked at the San Jacinto Battleground State Historical Park when I was home from college in the summer a few years ago. I never saw anything like this paper, but that doesn't mean much, because there is so much stuff there. The staff is incredible. There are some historians there who are incredibly knowledgeable. So if anyone can help you, it's them. The park is only about twenty miles east of Houston, just a beautiful place. And history is very rich there. The San Jacinto Volunteers even stage a reenactment of the battle each year in April. The battleship *Texas,* from World War I, is there on-site. And there's a huge monument that is just spectacular."

The Arlingtons were impressed.

"There's also a museum with thousands of items and even a huge collection of rare documents," Carolyn said. "I'll go right now and call ahead to Angela Amayo. She's a very nice woman, and I'd guess that she's been there at least twenty years."

The Arlingtons and Jane thanked her as she headed back inside.

Jane looked at her watch. "Looks like you'll have plenty of time," she said, smiling, "if you head out now."

The family agreed and made plans to touch base with Jane again the next day.

The drive went by quickly as the conversation centered on the vast amount of history they had learned in such a short period of time.

"Hey, I just thought of something," Adam said. "In the lobby of the hotel I picked up one of those travel pamphlets that had San Jacinto on the cover."

Adam read to the family about how the San Jacinto Monument is dedicated "to Heroes of the Battle of San Jacinto and all others who contributed to the independence of Texas." He also read that the monument is a 570-foot limestone shaft topped by a 34-foot, 220-ton star symbolizing the Lone Star Republic, and that the building is listed in the Guinness Book of World Records as the world's tallest stone column memorial. The San Jacinto Museum of History, according to the pamphlet, is housed in the 570-foot San Jacinto Monument, located "on the battlefield where Texas won its independence from Mexico on April 21, 1836," Adam noted as he flipped the page.

"Okay, here's what we might be looking for," he said. He read from the pamphlet, "The museum is a private, nonprofit, educational organization with a collection that spans more than four hundred years of early Texas history, from the Spanish conquest through Texas in the nineteenth century. Emphasis is on colonial Texas as a part of Mexico and the Republic of Texas. The collection contains more than 100,000 objects, 250,000 documents, 10,000 visual images, and a 35,000-volume rare book library."

The family agreed that the San Jacinto museum provided their best opportunity for finding another clue, or at least providing some direction.

When the monument came into sight, the Arlingtons were breathless. They stopped a worker, who said that Angela Amayo was in the museum. She was in the middle of a presentation but would be available in about thirty minutes and had apparently requested that the Arlingtons wait for her.

"Thanks," Mr. Arlington said to the worker who relayed the message. "We'll just look around."

"Cool," Ashley said. "Maybe we can learn a little more about this place." She picked up a handful of information and volunteered to read a short article summarizing the Battle of San Jacinto.

"The Battle of San Jacinto was on April 21, 1836," Ashley read.

"Not too long after the Alamo," Adam said. "And even closer in time to the Goliad Massacre."

Ashley nodded and continued reading:

Sam Houston and the meager army of Texas retreated eastward following the fall of the Alamo in the spring of 1836. The troops were becoming increasingly impatient to engage the enemy, however, by the time they reached Buffalo Bayou, a few miles southeast of present-day Houston. On the morning of April 19, the Texans crossed over and marched down the right bank of Buffalo Bayou to within half a mile of its confluence with the San Jacinto River. Here, the army prepared their defenses on the edge of a grove of trees. Their rear was protected by timber and the bayou, while before them was an open prairie. On the following morning, Mexican General Antonio Lopez de Santa Anna came marching across the prairie in battle array. A volley from the Texans' "Twin Sisters" artillery brought him to a sudden halt. Falling back to a clump of trees a quarter of a mile distant, Santa Anna formed a line of battle. Colonel Sidney Sherman, at the head of the Texas cavalry, charged the Mexican army but accomplished little except to inspire the Texans with fresh enthusiasm for the following day. The 21st of April dawned bright and beautiful. The Texas army totaled about 750 men. They faced over 1500 of the enemy, who were flushed with pride at the successful offenses they had mounted in the previous few weeks against the Texans. Early in the morning, Houston sent Deaf Smith, the celebrated Texas spy, with two or three men to destroy Vince's bridge, over which the Mexican army had passed, thus cutting off the enemy's only available escape. When Houston's long-awaited order to advance was given, the Texans did not hesitate. When within seventy yards the word "Fire!" was given, the Texan shouts of "Remember the Alamo!" and "Remember Goliad!" rang out along the entire line. Within a short time, 700 Mexicans were slain, with another 730 taken as prisoners. The battle for Texas was won. A panel on the side of the monument at San Jacinto today underscores the importance of the battle after more than a century and a half of reflection: "Measured by its results, San Jacinto was one of the decisive battles of the world. The freedom of Texas from Mexico won here led to annexation and to the

Mexican War, resulting in the acquisition by the United States of the states of Texas, New Mexico, Arizona, Nevada, California, Utah, and parts of Colorado, Wyoming, Kansas, and Oklahoma. Almost one-third of the present area of the American nation, nearly a million square miles of territory, changed sovereignty."

The sheer volume of land involved was mind-boggling to the Arlingtons.

"That shaped not just the history of Texas," Mr. Arlington commented, "but the entire country. Imagine, had these events not transpired the way they did, how different the results might be. It's almost hard to comprehend how much these battles—at the Alamo, at Goliad, and here at San Jacinto—meant to the entire history of the United States."

As he spoke a tall woman approached them.

"Hello, I'm Angela Amayo," she said. "And I'm guessing you folks are looking for me."

The Arlingtons introduced themselves, and Adam pulled out a copy of the paper for Angela.

"I can't . . ." Angela said. "I, I, I . . . I'm speechless. When I received the call this morning that you'd be coming down, I had no idea that it was about something of this magnitude. I thought you just had a question about history or wanted a tour. But this, now *this* is more than I could have ever imagined!"

Mr. Arlington took hold of her arm as Angela teetered.

"Are you all right?" his wife asked her.

Angela adjusted her glasses and righted herself. "I'm just shocked. Let's go have a seat. Can I get you all water to drink?"

The Arlingtons thanked her and accepted the offer. She brought out five bottles of water, setting Adam's paper with the two merged notes on a table. She opened her water as she sat down.

"This is—or at least it could be—something that I've heard mentioned several times," Ms. Amayo said. "You see, a lot of people have their own views of what happened. And there are certain gaps in several of the most famous Texas legends. In those cases—and there are many—some people choose to fill in their own theories or pass along what has been passed along through the generations. There are some tall tales out there that perhaps don't bear out very much truth. However, there are other stories that probably contain a good deal of actual history. And out of all of those thousands of pounds of stories likely comes a good few pounds of truth. Of course, we have no way of knowing unless it's documented. But that is the potential beauty of this discovery—it is historical documentation."

She read the paper again, rubbing at her temple as she pondered the possibilities.

"I have heard of something like this, though I had no idea that it existed on paper, to be completely honest with you," she said. "A descendant of Sam Houston's brought the subject of this to my attention in a very brief conversation maybe twenty-five or even more years ago. This woman said it had been passed along to her—and she said it was just a story handed down verbally—that a defender in a key battle had told a woman there during the battle that this person had a weapon of some sort stashed. We thought it to be the battle here, or at Goliad. In fact, I'm not even sure the Alamo was a part of the discussion, because it wasn't in the immediate area, really. But with that small amount of information, we were just never able to really pursue it.

"I don't want to get your hopes up, because this descendant of Sam Houston said it had all been told to her, and the only concrete proof she had was a tiny strip of old paper that made no sense and actually had no reference to the Alamo. She said she was merely trying to link the piece of paper—which I never saw—to what she had been told."

The family exchanged curious glances. Ms. Amayo continued. "Now, this is a long, long time ago that I heard this story, but certainly it stuck in my mind," she said. "I didn't have any concrete proof, and I urged her to contact the folks at the Alamo anyway. However, I never heard another word about it. When I talked to an acquaintance in the Daughters of the Republic of Texas, she said she had never been contacted. Perhaps it was a loose end that this Houston descendant was unable to make sense of, which is certainly understandable, considering the amount of time that had passed and the sketchy bit of information she had. So—what do you folks think? Would you like to head to the estate of Hannah Houston-Helgado—it's up in Huntsville, just up Interstate 45, north of here?"

Adam felt his heart racing. "That's where Sam Houston retired to!" Adam said.

"I can give you directions," Angela said.

"Could we do that, Dad?" Adam asked his father.

Mr. and Mrs. Arlington exchanged glances. Both agreed it would be a good idea.

"You could come along with us, right?" Ashley asked Ms. Amayo.

"Of course!" she said. "I wouldn't miss it for . . ."

Just then she was paged to go to the main information desk. She came back carrying a sheet of paper and what appeared to be a map. She was also wearing a look of disappointment.

"I have to head downtown for a very important meeting—I totally put it out of my mind with all the excitement as we talked," she said. "But here's a piece of paper with the estate address and directions, and here's a map to follow. She lives just on the outskirts of Huntsville. You'll get a kick out of Hannah. She is so positive and upbeat. She must be ninety years old by now. I wish I had a phone number so I could call ahead for you, but I don't. Her home is actually on many of the historical lists. However, she hasn't gotten out much the past fifteen years or so. I see her every few years at various functions, though it has been several years, I must admit. Please call me as soon as you know anything. Here's a business card with my home number on it. Don't hesitate to call me at home, regardless of the hour."

The Arlingtons thanked her and assured her they would do just that as soon as they learned something. They headed outside toward their car. Ashley suddenly stopped.

"What's going on?" Mr. Arlington asked.

Ashley was looking upward toward the monument.

"Something up there, sis?" Adam asked, as he too stopped with his mother and father.

"I don't know if it's what I see, so much as it's what I feel," Ashley said. "I guess I just want to draw a long breath and soak in as much of it as I can. I mean, we've been here only a week, but we'll take home enough memories for a lifetime."

"There might be even more memories when we get to the Houston estate in Huntsville," Adam said. "Then again, who knows? We've come this far and have already learned a lot. Plus we've met some awesome people we won't forget for the rest of our lives."

The Arlingtons took their time, surveying the area for a few minutes.

"Do you wonder?" Ashley asked out loud.

"About what?" Mrs. Arlington asked.

Ashley looked toward her family. "All of this history," she said. "What if all of these heroes hadn't had the courage to defend the Alamo, to fight through the painful knowledge of the Goliad Massacre . . . to lay it all on the line here at San Jacinto?"

The family moved closer to each other.

"I think it involves more than the actual map of what became the United States—it's what became the spirit that lives on in Texas," Mrs. Arlington said. "There are certain events in history that simply can't ever be forgotten. These events have made Texas—made all of us Americans—who we are today."

The family headed to the car. After a short stop to refuel and get some drive-through lunch, they headed to the Houston suburb.

It was only 3:00, so they had plenty of time. They found their exit and headed toward the Houston estate in Huntsville. Angela Amayo's directions were perfect. At the gate, they stopped and buzzed.

"May I help you?" a voice asked.

"My name is Alex Arlington," Mr. Arlington said. "I'm

here from Washington, D.C., with my wife and our children. We're here to see Hannah Houston-Helgado."

There was a long pause.

"Mrs. Houston-Helgado is not here," the voice said.

Mr. Arlington peered toward the backseat.

"Ask when she'll be back," Ashley whispered.

He did. But the answer wasn't what he was looking for.

"Mrs. Houston-Helgado will not be returning," the voice said.

"Today, or ever?" he asked.

"Never," the voice said. "Please have a good day. Good-bye."

Great-great Uncle Sam

"Never!" Adam proclaimed. "Um, Mom . . . Dad, say something!"

"Excuse me, excuse me!" Mr. Arlington called out. "Please!"

There was a twenty-second pause.

"If you don't leave the premises, you will be escorted away by sheriff's deputies," the voice said. "You are now considered to be trespassing on private property. Please leave before we summon the authorities."

Mrs. Arlington stared at the box. She then leaned toward the window.

"We're not here to cause trouble or trespass or harass anyone," she said, thinking quickly. She motioned toward Adam and whispered, "Give me a copy of the sheet with the note on it."

Adam quickly obliged.

"We have a copy of a note that might be something sent to Sam Houston, or to or from an Alamo defender," she yelled toward the box. "We will leave it here, at the base of the gate, and we'll put a rock on it to hold it down until you get out here. Please, though, get it to Mrs. Houston-Helgado. We've been told that she might be the only person in this country who might appreciate or understand its historical value. Call Angela Amayo at the San Jacinto Battleground Museum—she'll tell you that we're here in regard to a very meaningful cause."

There was a long pause—a really long one this time. In fact, almost five minutes passed. Mr. Arlington looked in the rearview mirror toward the backseat again.

"Well," he said, "we probably should leave, because if we don't, we'll have trouble with the authorities."

Adam grabbed the front seat and pulled himself up to it.

"No, Dad! Please, no!" Adam said. "We've come so far . . . we could be so close."

Mrs. Arlington put her hands on the hands of her son.

"Listen, Adam, I completely understand how you feel," she said. "But . . . "

Just then came a series of several clicks over the box. There was another series of four clicks, and after what seemed like hours but was less than a minute, on came a voice. But this was not the same voice of the young woman from earlier. This was definitely a much older woman.

"Good day," the voice said. "I do, indeed, know Angela. Please, as soon as the gate opens, enter the grounds and pull up to the main house. You will be met at the two wooden front doors. Thank you, and welcome."

Adam sighed and leaned back, bouncing his head off the seat. Ashley hugged him in excitement.

"Wow!" Ashley said. "That was a close one."

Their parents chuckled. "Way closer than I ever wanted," their mom said, laughing.

"Me too," said their dad. "I could see the newspaper headline back home, 'Local attorney busted scaling fence of elderly Houston namesake's home.'"

"Or the TV news," Ashley said. "Surely there are security cameras here. It would be like, 'That's the backside of local lawyer Alex Arlington as he illegally enters . . . More film at eleven.'"

Everyone laughed except Adam. "You'd have done that, Dad?" he asked incredulously.

Mrs. Arlington looked at her husband, knowing—or at least hoping—his better judgment would have prevailed even as emotions heated up.

"Oh, maybe I wouldn't have gone that far. It certainly isn't worth breaking the law over," he said. "On the other hand, we'd have probably gone ourselves to the local police to have her contacted for us. Or we could have gotten Angela to come back with us. We'd have done something, let's put it that way."

The winding road up to the spacious house was beautiful. The grounds were manicured, and various sculptures and fountains dotted the lawn and the side of the long driveway.

As they pulled up to the house, a younger woman came out. The Arlingtons climbed out of the car, and Mrs. Arlington introduced the family while extending her hand to the woman.

"I'm Mrs. Houston-Helgado's assistant, Angie," the woman said. "I was the first one you talked to."

The Arlingtons recognized her voice.

"I apologize for trying to shoo you away," Angie said. "It's just that we get a lot of tourists and pranks here, and we can't be coming out for all of them, much less inviting people into the house. But you've certainly piqued Mrs. Houston-Helgado's interest, so we'll head into the foyer to wait for her. She's still a live wire, even at ninety. And let me tell you that her eyes really lit up when she heard why you were here."

Adam pulled out a copy of the note and handed it to her.

"So did she say that it made some sort of sense to her?" he asked.

"No, she didn't say anything," Angie answered.

"Does this look like anything familiar to you?" Ashley asked. "Maybe you've seen a piece of paper that looks like this note? An old piece of paper, sort of ripped?"

Angie pursed her lips together and shook her head side to side.

"Young man, I wish it did look familiar," Angie said, looking up, "especially now that I see that look on your face."

Adam grinned sheepishly.

"Let's head into the house," she said, opening a large iron handle.

As they walked into the front door, an elderly woman came toward them. "I'm Hannah Houston-Helgado," she said, extending her hand toward Mrs. Arlington.

The Arlingtons were surprised that Hannah was moving so quickly, taking long, quick strides toward them.

"I'm very excited to meet you," she said.

"I'm Anne Arlington, and this is my husband, Alex, and our children, Ashley and Adam," Mrs. Arlington said.

Adam quickly fished another copy of the note out of his backpack.

"This is for you, Mrs. Houston-Helgado," he said.

"Please, everyone, call me Hannah," she said. Hannah had her glasses on a string around her neck. She placed the paper Adam had handed her under her elbow, and pulled the glasses on. "Angie, if you have to get back to work, I understand."

"I'm a distant relative, and I assist her in managing all of her business affairs," Angie said. "Our accounting firm represents her, and I really enjoy the time we spend together. But I had best get back to work."

Angie excused herself.

Hannah stared and stared at the paper Adam had handed her, and didn't say a word. Then she pressed her lips together and appeared to force a hard swallow.

"Goodness," she said softly, "and after all of these years, who'd have thought it . . . "

They could barely hear her.

"Is everything all right, Hannah?" Mrs. Arlington asked. "Are you sure you're okay?"

Hannah turned toward her and smiled broadly. She asked, "May I?" and reached for her arm, which Mrs. Arlington gladly extended.

"Let's retreat to the study," she said, "if you don't mind lending me a little help."

Adam quickly stepped to the other side and offered his arm for Hannah's other hand, which she gladly accepted.

"I don't know if you're going to believe all of this," Hannah said, "but this . . . this could really complete a part of my life that has kind of been dangling. You might be able to close the circle for me."

Adam raised his eyebrows toward Ashley, who smiled excitedly.

"Well, Hannah," Ashley said, touching the woman's back gently with her hand, "you might be able to help us close a circle too, one that started very unexpectedly with just a little note."

Hannah smiled and motioned for the family to sit on a leather couch and matching chairs in a spacious study. The room was wooden, including the floor, though several throw rugs—which looked to be of the same motif as the quilts the Arlingtons had picked up at the flea market—dotted the floor.

There were several small paintings, and one large one behind a grand desk. Hannah deftly slid out of her chair to the desk and sat down.

"Does anyone recognize this man behind me?" Hannah asked, raising her head upward and back.

Mr. and Mrs. Arlington looked at each other. They both had a guess but weren't sure. Adam was sure, however.

"Ma'am, that's the legendary Sam Houston," Adam said proudly.

Hannah again smiled broadly.

"That's my great-great Uncle Sam," Hannah said, looking toward the Arlingtons. "Get it?—Uncle Sam!"

The Arlingtons laughed.

"That's always good for a chuckle," Hannah said. "But he really is my great-great uncle. And I'm so proud of him."

"I'm proud of him too, and he's not even my uncle," Ashley said, "because without him and the men he led, I don't know if Texas and the rest of the territory he helped the U.S. get would belong to our country today."

Hannah smiled appreciatively as she picked up the note and studied it. She held it up with her left hand.

"This has been something that has troubled me for the better part of half a century," Hannah said. "But now, it all makes sense. I'm so thankful you are here today."

"We're thankful too," Adam said.

Hannah stood.

"Well, this is a very big moment," Hannah said. "Do you see that frame?"

She pointed toward the bottom right corner of the huge painting of Sam Houston. Its picture frame had a very old document inside it, along with his portrait. The frame was sealed, with giant keyholes on the corner.

"Is that picture," Adam said as he stood and walked toward it, "locked up? I've never seen a frame that does that before."

"Oh yes," Hannah said. "But this is very valuable. Even the glass isn't breakable. This is very precious."

The Arlingtons could see an older document within the frame, though it was obviously not part of the note.

"Cool!" Ashley said as she looked more closely. "It's part of the Texas Declaration of Independence."

Putting the Pieces Together

Adam peered closer.

"This is just a part of the middle of the Declaration," Hannah said. "Let me read it to you."

Nations, as well as individuals, are amenable for their acts to the public opinion of mankind. A statement of a part of our grievances is therefore submitted to an impartial world, in justification of the hazardous but unavoidable step now taken, of severing our political connection with the Mexican people, and assuming an independent attitude among the nations of the earth. The Mexican government, by its colonization laws, invited and induced the Anglo-American population of Texas to colonize its wilderness under the pledged faith of a written constitution, that they should continue to enjoy that constitutional liberty and republican government to which they had been habituated in the land of their birth, the United States of America. In this expectation they have been cruelly disappointed, inasmuch as the Mexican nation has acquiesced in the late changes made in the government by General Antonio Lopez de Santa Anna, who having overturned the constitution of his country, now offers us the cruel alternative, either to abandon our homes, acquired by so many privations, or submit to the most intolerable of all tyranny, the combined despotism of the sword and the priesthood.

The Arlingtons were amazed at the hands-on history lesson they were getting about this state that had them so intrigued—and even smitten—because of the Texans' incredible spirit and independence.

"Sam Houston's signature is on this document," Adam said.

"That's correct," Hannah said, "though it's not on this copy. You can go see the original, or see it on the Internet."

Adam also remembered what he had read about Sam Houston.

"After this was posted, he was elected the first governor of the Republic of Texas," Adam said. "Then later he was elected as a congressman from Texas, and finally a governor of the state of Texas. When he disagreed with Texas's decision to secede from the Union in 1861, that was pretty much the end of his political career."

Ashley found all of this enthralling but didn't quite understand how it was linked to the note they were tracking down. "That's nice, Adam, but how does that help us with our search?"

"Well, this is why you're all here," Hannah said. "Once again, I want to thank you all."

She opened the locked drawer and then pulled out a small lockbox. From there, she pulled out a set of small keys. She sighed and set them down.

"Would one of you mind carefully doing this for me?" Hannah said. "I'll coach you, but I'm afraid my hands aren't cooperating today."

The Arlingtons smiled. Both of the kids wanted the honor. However, Mr. Arlington nodded toward Adam, and Ashley smiled at him. She knew he was the one who had gotten this whole thing started.

"So you think we're close?" Adam asked.

"To what?" Hannah said with a smile.

"To finding the missing part of the note," Adam said. "I'm just worried about opening this, because I'm not certain how the Texas Declaration of Independence fits in."

Hannah placed her hands on Adam's shoulders.

"It will make sense in a minute," Hannah said. "I figured it out the moment I read the piece of paper you handed me. Certainly, I took you on a circuitous route, but I hope you enjoyed the history lesson."

Adam turned toward Hannah. "Oh yes, ma'am!" he said. "I wouldn't trade it for anything, and I was just trying to see how this fit in."

"Well, then," Hannah smiled at his enthusiasm, "just undo these locks very, very carefully."

Adam did, and the back of the frame was unhinged from the solid wood board. On the back was a piece of thick, red felt. On the front, within a neatly trimmed and stitched frame made by the piece of felt, was the Declaration.

"Careful now, hon," Hannah said. "Stand it on its side, and carefully pull up, from the back, the piece of felt."

Adam stood the frame up, with the Declaration facing forward and the back of the frame facing him. A piece of laminated paper slipped off the frame and onto the desk.

"The other part of the note!" Adam cried out.

"Okay now," Mr. Arlington said, "keep your head and your focus, and put that frame back together again. Is that all right, Hannah?"

She nodded yes. "That would be perfect," she said. "Just put it back together, making sure the felt lines up, and lock it up. What fell out just now isn't going back in—at least not in that frame."

Adam paid attention to what he was doing, folding the felt back in exactly how he'd found it. He secured the locks and handed the keys to Hannah, who, while Adam put the frame back on the wall, put the keys back in the lock-box and into the drawer.

Ashley picked up the piece of laminated paper and handed it to Hannah.

"This story has been handed down through generations in my family, but with only this little bit of information, we were never able to make anything out of it," Hannah said. "We knew it was a part of a letter written to Sam Houston. Apparently, after it was written, someone else got ahold of it and tore it once, or maybe even twice. This part of it was all that was salvaged, so we had no idea that the other parts still existed—or even how to go about finding out. We had heard that there might be a Tejano descendant who had some knowledge of the letter, but with such sketchy information, it never led anywhere."

Adam thought about it for a second.

"I'll bet you Gregorio Esparza wrote it—we kind of know that—and then when it got torn for whatever reason, the only part he saved is what he stitched into the holster," Adam said. "Of course, we don't have enough information to say that's exactly what happened, but it's a good guess."

Ashley agreed.

"And perhaps Mr. Moreno's relative was the one who tore it," Ashley hypothesized, "and he kept it, maybe having second thoughts about disposing of it and realizing it was important enough to pass along. We're talking about a Texan, a Tejano, and a Mexican, so there were three very noble—but very separate—causes in many ways."

Hannah was impressed. "And whoever had the third piece thought enough to mail it to Sam Houston," she said. "But the piece never reached him, because he had already moved to Huntsville when the piece of mail was delivered in 1870. The postmark was August 1, 1863."

"It just missed reaching Sam Houston!" Adam said. "Because he died in July of 1863, if I remember it right."

"You remember correctly," Hannah said. "This envelope was passed around and wasn't even opened until it was finally retrieved or somehow sent to the next generation of Houstons. They didn't really know what to make of it, so it was kept with a bunch of other old mementos—many that probably had some history, but we knew nothing about it. I always felt some sort of affection for this note and hoped to find out something about it. Whenever I pursued it, though, I came up completely empty-handed. So, I guess when I was about sixty, I sort of gave up. We did donate the envelope to the museum, the one at San Jacinto, in fact."

"That's where we were today!" Adam said. "We must've been within a few feet of it at some point."

"Maybe," Hannah said. "I took the envelope down there to donate it almost thirty years ago. It had a San Jacinto postmark, so I thought it would make a good addition to the museum. That postmark is why I thought the note had to be related to either Goliad or San Jacinto. The Alamo never really crossed my mind as a possibility. I tried to track down some information about the paper. It was so brittle by then, of course, that I didn't take it along. I had it professionally preserved and laminated, and I put it in the back of this frame."

Ashley looked up. "And that's where you met Angela Amayo!" she said.

"Why, that's correct," Hannah said.

She was still holding the paper with both hands. "Oh my, how rude of me!" she proclaimed with a smile. "You kids must be screaming inside to see what this says!"

Adam and Ashley just laughed.

"I think they're more than just a little curious," Mr. Arlington said with a grin.

Adam grabbed his backpack and started to unzip it. He paused. "Is it okay if I take a picture of that?" he asked, pointing toward the laminated note.

"Certainly," Hannah said. "Now here, I'll set it down, and your puzzle will be complete."

She set it on the table that was in the center of the room. Mr. and Mrs. Arlington leaned forward on the couch, while Ashley and Adam stood.

Adam read it to the group.

to find these two six-shooters. They were packed in the sod by the well, about a foot behind the handle, where they wouldn't be stepped on. That way, if he were either forced to or allowed to get water, he could retrieve the weapons, which I believe are loaded. I was given the holster by someone who attended to him in the very end.

God's Glory to you . . . GE

"Surely 'GE' must be Gregorio Esparza!" Ashley said.

"No doubt about that," Mr. Arlington agreed.

"So that means the holster I have really is from the Alamo—and it once belonged to James Bowie!" Adam cried out.

Hannah and the Arlingtons looked at each other. Mrs. Arlington explained that this whole mystery had started with the holster.

"Surely there's a very, very good chance that you are correct, young man," Hannah said.

Adam gathered the piece of paper and the laminated note.

"Hannah, can you take the other parts of the note and please be the first one to read it in its entirety? You know, you will be the first person in 140 years to do that," Adam said.

Hannah had a lump in her throat.

"That's quite an honor," Hannah said. "And while you two wonderful kids have earned the right to do that, I am blessed and thankful. I will gladly read it."

She rubbed softly at her eyes and then picked up the copy Adam had given her, holding her part of the note at the bottom. She read the note, the first time it had been read in its entirety since the dusty days of the past. It had not survived a possible tussle between friends whole, but since each of the parts had survived the time and elements since then, it was, at last, united in its entirety.

Houston, it is of my belief that he was worried that he would be captured because of his growing incapacity, which he fought at every step just as vigorously as he fought in battle. And if captured, on the chance that he could get free, he would have access to those right away. He really thought he could take them all alone, even if he were the last man standing, did he not? So he battled to the end, and by stowing those, he could still defend the Alamo in honor, at least

that was his thought. Yet if they are looking for an edge, they will miss the target. JB knew better; that is why he did it. He anticipated the attack two weeks early, even though he was ill and getting worse. But I assume they are still there. Do not fail to remember that we are the only two who have knowledge of this. This is a link to San Jacinto, to Goliad. You understand that as a Tejano, I have an obligation

to find these two six-shooters. They were packed in the sod by the well, about a foot behind the handle, where they wouldn't be stepped on. That way, if he were either forced to or allowed to get water, he could retrieve the weapons, which I believe are loaded. I was given the holster by someone who attended to him in the very end.

God's Glory to you . . . GE

"Amazing!" Adam called out. "Just incredible!"

Hannah also had a stunned look on her face. "It sounds like this is part of the Alamo's history," she said.

Ashley stood and peered at the note. Adam took a picture of Hannah's portion of it.

"What I don't understand," Ashley said, "is exactly how the note was torn and ended up in its different places. I know we have some good theories, and the information we have does at least partially support the way we think it happened, but how do we know for sure?"

Hannah sat down on the couch and pulled Ashley down next to her. "You know, hon, that's been the story of my life in chasing my family's history," Hannah said thoughtfully. "To be sure, some of the history is very, very well-documented, and there is little problem validating a series of events, names, or places. But in other instances, there are gaps. It's hard to fill those in. Let me tell you that for what you all had to work with, you did an outstanding job. I can't think of anyone else who has taken such a cold, long-forgotten trail and put it together like this. You could take a team of the best detectives in the country and they'd have a hard time matching the job you and your brother, and your parents, of course, did with this letter."

Ashley knew in her heart that Hannah was exactly right. She recalled hearing about how even the events at the Alamo still had some questions surrounding them in certain cases.

"Besides, sis," Adam said, "we have all three pieces now. We've got the note. But there's something else to get—the guns!"

Mr. Arlington put up his hands to caution his son. "Whoa, Adam, we don't know that they are even there," he said. "The Alamo has undergone a lot of restoration and changes. I'd be very surprised if the guns haven't already been discovered or possibly even been taken away by now. And if they are there, they'd have sat for 145 years. What are the odds of the guns still being there? Think about it."

Adam pondered the thought. "I think about 75 percent," he said.

Hannah and Mr. and Mrs. Arlington smiled at each other.

"That might be way too optimistic," Mrs. Arlington said. "Do you realize that?"

"What do you think the chances are, Mom?" Adam asked. "And you too, Hannah?"

Hannah nodded toward Mrs. Arlington to answer first.

"Maybe 1 percent," his mother said. She knew by the look on Adam's and Ashley's faces that that wasn't the answer they had been looking for.

Search for the Six-shooters

Hannah paused. "I think it's closer to 50 percent," she said, immediately perking the look on the kids' faces. "I don't know how to say otherwise—better or worse. They might be there, they might not. I take it you folks already have a contact at the Alamo?"

"Oh yes," Adam said. "Her name is Jane Jermillo. We have her number, and of course you can have it."

Hannah pulled a pad from the desk. As she did, Adam picked up her piece of the letter.

"Where would you like to keep this now?" Adam asked.

"Well, I hadn't thought about that," Hannah said. "You don't want to take it with you?"

Adam looked toward his parents. They shrugged their shoulders, which Adam took as implying he could make the decision.

"We sort of made it part of our 'mission' to not disturb history," Adam said. "You know, the theory of going into a wilderness and leaving only the lightest of footprints—

not disturbing anything. Putting it back would keep that going. I have a picture of it, actually about twenty pictures! So I'll put together all three pieces on my computer. I can enhance the paper to preserve the historical quality of it—the way it shows it's worn with time and so on—and then I'll get you a copy."

Hannah thought all of that sounded good.

"Are we forgetting anything?" Mrs. Arlington asked the kids. "What's next?"

Ashley and Adam exchanged glances. Ashley knew what her mother meant.

"We'd like to know what you would be comfortable with, Hannah, about what's done next," Ashley said. "We don't want to step on anyone's toes. I think we would like to take a copy of the whole note back to Jane Jermillo and, probably tomorrow morning instead of today, see what the folks at the Alamo think."

The Arlingtons were proud that their daughter had the right perspective.

"That sounds wonderful," Hannah said. "Just keep me up-to-date if there are any developments. I must admit, I am more excited and eager to leave these grounds than I have been in a long time. If there is anything else you need, let me know. I can have Angie drive me to San Antonio if you need me there."

The Arlingtons noticed it was getting late, and they didn't want to impose on Hannah's time much longer.

"We'll call you as soon as we talk to Jane, if that's all right," Adam said.

Hannah put an arm around each of the kids as she walked them toward the front door.

"I don't know if you realize how much you've done for me today," Hannah said. "This was one of the big question marks—one of the few, really—left in my life. I won't be around forever. To have you kids uncover a part of history that has been dormant for so long says a lot about you two and how you've been raised."

The Arlingtons exchanged hugs with Hannah, then headed to their car and pulled away.

The car was abuzz the whole way back to San Antonio. Once in Austin, the family stopped for gas and food, and then made the final part of the jaunt to San Antonio.

Sure enough, the Alamo was closed when they got back, as it was well past 9:00 P.M. But Mr. Arlington suggested Adam or Ashley call Jane at her cell number.

"Is it okay to call her this late?" Adam asked.

"I think the circumstances warrant it," Mrs. Arlington assured him.

"Here, Ash," Adam said, handing his sister the phone number, "you're way better at this kind of thing—you do it."

Ashley laughed and took the number.

"Hi, Jane, this is Ashley Arlington; I apologize for calling you so late," Ashley said. "We found the other piece of the note! Turns out that it does, for sure, involve the Alamo. It talks about a set of six-shooters that James Bowie stored by the well in the sod, in case he was captured."

"Fantastic!" Jane exclaimed on the other end of the line. She was so loud, in fact, that Adam and his parents also heard her and smiled. "Hey, I'll be right by. I have a contact, Dr. Thomas, at the University of Texas in Austin who has a machine that x-rays through material and even ground—sod, earth, mud, you name it. Maybe I can get him there at sunup tomorrow morning before we open, and we can find out something."

After Ashley's conversation with Jane, Adam went to the hotel office and downloaded his picture of Hannah's part of the note. He brought the file in with the other two pieces of the note and reconstructed it in its entirety. While it certainly wasn't exactly like it had been almost 150 years earlier, it was still impressive. The first thing he did was save a couple of copies of the note to a pair of disks, and then he e-mailed it to his sister, himself, and his parents. He wanted to make sure that no matter what happened, he would always have access to a copy of it.

Again he printed out multiple copies, then he headed back up to the hotel room. Though he was only downstairs fifteen minutes, Jane was already in their room. Adam quickly passed out copies of the note, and Ashley had already brought Jane up to speed on how the day's events had unfolded.

"This might be the most amazing piece of living history—come-to-life history, if you will—that I've ever seen!" Jane said. "I'll make sure we're all over it first thing in the morning. I don't know that the six-shooters would still be there. I'm thinking about the well—and there are a couple of small rises on each side of it—but after all of these years, I wonder if there's even a chance that those guns would be there? Surely by now someone would've found them, I think. But we'll call you if we uncover anything."

Ashley and Adam's crestfallen looks caught Jane's attention.

"How silly of me!" Jane said. "You all are invited, about 4:30 A.M., if you'd like. It'll be quite brisk out, and barely light. I just thought you might want to sleep in after doing so much work and covering so much ground—and history—today."

Adam stood up. "I'd go down there now and sleep at the gates if my parents would let me," he said.

"Luckily, your parents are smarter than that," his mother replied, standing to walk Jane to the door. "We'll be there, bright and early. Thanks so much for coming so quickly on such short notice."

"Thanks!" Adam and Ashley called out in unison.

"No, thank *you!*" Jane said. "This is about the most exciting thing that has happened in a good, long spell. Can't wait till morning!"

She headed out the door, and Mr. Arlington walked her to the elevator, downstairs, and out to her car.

Ashley and Adam fell asleep quickly, which was a good thing; they were up not even seven hours later to head to the Alamo. They quickly grabbed pieces of fruit and ate while they walked.

They turned the corner and saw a huge machine already set up by the well.

"Hi!" Jane said. "We're about ready to start."

The expert from the University of Texas, Dr. Steve Thomas, introduced himself and several of the half-dozen or so staff members he had brought along. A good dozen or so of the Alamo staff and Daughters of the Republic of Texas had also assembled.

Dr. Thomas scanned with his machine to the left of the well, and it turned up nothing. "Not a single thing," he said. "There's nothing in here, I can tell you that for certain."

Digging In

"That's okay," Adam said to Jane. "It's supposed to be on the other side, by the handle."

"I know," Jane whispered to Adam and Ashley, "but I thought since they were already here, I'd have them run it by the other side just in case you and your sister come back on vacation next year!"

They all shared a big laugh. Dr. Thomas then went to the other side of the well. There was no visible reaction from the machine as he ran it along the top of the small mound.

Suddenly the machine hummed wildly. Thomas stuck his head against a small video screen. "Metal!" he yelled. "Two large clumps of metal, maybe a foot or so long each!"

Adam and Ashley started jumping in the air.

"This doesn't mean it is necessarily a pair of guns," Thomas cautioned. "Then again, I'd have no reason to bet against it. Jane, when could we dig into this thing? I mean,

I'm sure you have to go up the chain of command and through several channels to get permission."

"I already have permission," Jane said, waving an envelope. "And we have more than five hours until we open at ten. If it goes longer, we can rope it off and get security in here to surround it."

Thomas studied the screen a little longer and jotted down a few notes. "We won't need a backhoe or anything, or even a jackhammer. I think, though it might take an hour or two, that we could get to it with a shovel at first, and then spades and spoons as we get closer. Our data shows the bodies of mass to be about thirty or so inches in if we go from this side," he said.

Ashley and Adam were standing back out of the way. They watched as Jane pulled Dr. Thomas aside.

When they came back, he addressed Ashley and Adam.

"Well, it appears you two are the ones who got us to this point," Thomas said. "My excavators will go in, but we'll be asking for your help. You'll have to listen closely and do exactly what you're told—if you see something, you can't jerk it out of the dirt. But if that sounds all right, Jane would like to have you on the team with my staff."

"Awesome," Adam said. "Thanks a lot!"

Dr. Thomas motioned them toward his truck. "Get into gear," he said. "You'll put on the same one-piece utility suit that we're wearing, and of course the gloves. Then just stand by until we call you in."

"Got it," Ashley said.

The two went and got dressed. Because there was a level of stone over the mound, it had to be carefully chipped away first. At that point, several of Thomas's staff members dug in gently, taking away small shovels of dirt. They took about a foot off of the mound, working very deliberately.

Then Dr. Thomas set up his machine again.

"Less than a foot," he said, cupping his hands around the side of his eyes to view the screen on the machine since the sun was out, creating a glare. "Let's go at it with the small tools. Detail team, let's go."

Adam and Ashley wanted to jump in the air again, but instead they just grasped each other's hands firmly.

"Hey!" Thomas said loudly toward Adam and Ashley. "Are you two in or out?"

Adam and Ashley carefully stepped over the cord set up to cordon off the area. Thomas handed them each a small fiberglass spade.

"Soft, soft, soft," Thomas said, showing them how as he gently scooped about a tablespoon of dirt away, "and then peer in to see if you can establish a visual with whatever's in there."

They worked for an hour, and it seemed like they were still miles, not inches, away. Thomas had a couple of his own staff take over for Adam and Ashley.

"It's nerve-racking, isn't it?" Thomas said with a smile. "I'd be more relaxed and less exhausted drilling a four-hundred-foot tunnel than going after an artifact."

Ashley and Adam stood and talked to their parents and Jane as they sipped water. It was warming up outside, and it was almost 8:30 when Thomas motioned again.

"Let's go, kids," Thomas said. "We have visual!"

Adam and Ashley looked. All they could see was part of what appeared to be a potato sack.

"We'll all work together," Thomas said. "Let's remove these, but only after we've completely cleared all the dirt off—we'll use the softest brushes on the top when we get to that point."

With every grain of dirt that was either shoveled away with a spoon or brushed away with one of Thomas's brushes, more and more of the potato sack was visible.

"I can't believe this!" Jane whispered excitedly to Mr. and Mrs. Arlington. "And your kids are a part of this! This has turned out to be quite a vacation, hasn't it? Might you come back again?"

"I think you can count on that," Mr. Arlington said with a chuckle. "I think our kids already want to move here."

Adam and Ashley stopped removing dirt. The top of the bag was visible. There were two large objects inside, one with a long, hard piece of metal on top. When the sack was removed, they'd be able to find out what the bottom object was.

"I'll get that," Thomas said, positioning himself so he'd place no stress on the bag. He had a small tray and carefully took hold of the bag. He instructed a member of his team to get on each side, so there would be no jostling of whatever was in the sack as they put it on the tray.

"Okay if we open it out here?" Thomas asked.

Jane stared toward the sky. "I don't see any precipitation now, or any on the way," she said. Adam and Ashley noticed the deep blue of the sky.

"I was hoping it wouldn't rain on this special day," Ashley whispered to her brother.

"Boy, and is it a special day!" Adam replied.

Unpacking Bowie's Bag

Dr. Thomas turned with the tray and gently placed it on a table that had been set up earlier a few feet in front of the well on the stone walkway.

"There it is," he said. "Jane, would you like to handle the honor?"

The look on Jane's face said it all. She was more than excited and enthralled that the Alamo was coming to life once again. But as she gently touched the sack, she stopped.

"No, this wouldn't be right," Jane said. "I'll help. But, Ashley and Adam, I'll need you up here to help me. While Dr. Thomas and his crew have done an outstanding job— for which I'm very grateful—we wouldn't be here today if it weren't for these two special teens."

Mrs. Arlington had been holding Ashley's hand, and Mr. Arlington had his arm around Adam. The teens looked at their parents for approval.

"We really aren't part of this—we aren't the owners or even Texans," Ashley said. "We'd love to, Ms. Jermillo, but we don't want to intrude on history."

Jane turned and reached out her arm.

"I appreciate your kind words and the thoughts behind them," Jane said. "But if you two don't come up here, I'm not going to open this!"

"Come on, Ashley and Adam!" Dr. Thomas said. "Let's get this over with!"

Mr. and Mrs. Arlington gently nudged their children forward.

Jane had Adam on her right and Ashley on her left.

"You two stabilize this as I open the sack," Jane said, noticing it was stitched all the way around. "It's only tied off on this side, but it's double-stitched on the other side. So I'll just cut the stitching on the top end, and we'll go from there."

Jane unsheathed a knife from her belt and carefully clipped the end. She opened the sack, and a clump of dust plumed out. She crouched down and peeked into the sack, where no one else could see. She turned it to face the other way—away from everyone.

"That's my part done," Jane said. "There are two in there. Ashley and Adam, would you each—very carefully, of course—take one out? Remember, these might still have bullets in the chambers."

Adam motioned for Ashley to go first.

"But you started this search," Ashley protested.

"Yes, but you helped get it going, and you've been there at every step," Adam said. "I'll get the last one—I'll finish it."

Jane again opened the sack, this time a little wider. Ashley looked in and saw two dirty pieces of metal or wood. She chose to remove the top one, so as not to have the top one slip or get nicked if she pulled out the bottom one first.

Adam held the top of the sack, and Ashley removed the first of what turned out to be two guns. The barrel was long, though the white handles were in a state of disrepair. Still, as Adam pulled out the other, the effects of the weather, dirt, and time did nothing to take away from the majesty of the moment.

"Wow!" Adam said quietly. "I can't believe it! Six-shooters."

On the handle of the one Ashley was holding, though dirty, was clearly the letter *J*. Adam saw that letter on the gun Ashley was holding and looked at his own. And there it was, a *B*.

"James Bowie!" Ashley said. "Just as you thought, Adam, all along!"

"He really did think he could take them, didn't he?" Adam said, feeling his eyes start to get watery. "Bowie was going to do all he could to defend the Alamo. I didn't know him, but I'm so proud of him."

"And he once held these very guns; there's little doubt about that!" Jane said.

"Awesome!" Adam said. "It was victory or death. Our heroes met with their death. But it led to a greater victory after what happened at Goliad and then at San Jacinto."

Jane motioned toward Dr. Thomas, who was ready to take the guns.

Remembering a lesson their father had taught them years ago, the Arlington kids carefully turned the guns in their hands barrel first, so as to not point the guns at Thomas as they handed them over to him.

Thomas tapped gently on the sides of the guns and told everyone that both were loaded. He looked closer and using a toothpick poked into the chambers, where the guns were loaded.

"Six bullets in each," Thomas said. "Just like it said in the note. Loaded six-shooters."

Jane knew what had to be done next.

"From a historical perspective, it would be best to leave them loaded, as we found them," she said. "But on the other hand, it would be safer to get the bullets out. That way, we can display each gun here along with its six bullets."

Thomas and his staff worked with great care and patience to unload the guns. It wasn't easy because of all the dirt. And because they didn't want to inflict any further wear or tear on the weapons, it took almost thirty-five minutes to remove the bullets.

"I'm going to get a case for these," Jane said. "We have one here that will be perfect. No sense in waiting. I'm so excited to show these to visitors of the Alamo! Thank you, kids!"

She pulled off her gloves and squeezed a cheek on Adam's and Ashley's faces. They blushed. But they were also exuberant. They hugged their parents.

"You kids must be awfully proud," Mr. Arlington said, "because we sure are very proud of you two."

When Jane came back with the case, Dr. Thomas was working on making the guns presentable.

"I could take these back to the lab and get them looking a little better," Thomas said. "But of course it's your call, you and the Daughters of the Republic of Texas."

"I think they look great like they are," Jane said. "Plus with the copy of the note that Adam and Ashley made on their computer by compiling the three original pieces of the letter on display, we can tell our guests at the Alamo about the story behind the story and how these weapons were found."

Mr. and Mrs. Arlington moved closer to Jane.

"We know you have a lot of work to do now," Mrs. Arlington said, "and you're getting ready to open the Alamo. We're going to get out of your way. But thanks so much for letting our family be a part of it."

Jane hugged Mr. and Mrs. Arlington.

"Thanks to all of you!" she said. "You kids are the ones who let *me* get involved in this, and I will always be grateful. I'm going to talk to the others in the chain of command here, and we'll set up a ceremony to dedicate these tomorrow. I'd like to get your other friends here—Mr. Esparza, Mr. Moreno, Hannah Houston-Helgado, Angela Amayo, and of course Mike Martinez."

"Oh no!" Adam said. "We have no way of contacting Mr. Esparza."

Mr. Arlington looked at his wife. He didn't have a good answer. "That's true," he said. "But we know Mr. Martinez pretty well, and I'm sure Hannah would love to come down."

Jane started to walk the Arlingtons toward the gate. "I'll be right back, Steve," she said. Dr. Thomas nodded.

The Arlingtons walked slowly, taking in every possible piece of the moment.

"Listen, could you call Martinez, Hannah, and Angela?" Jane said.

The Arlingtons nodded.

"I think Adam will call Martinez and Angela, and Ashley can call Hannah," Mrs. Arlington said.

"That's great," Jane said. "Hey, Adam and Ashley, I'm going to put out a press release for this. I can guarantee you this place will be crazy tomorrow with media. We won't announce it to the public, just because of security concerns. But we'll have everyone from the Daughters of the Republic of Texas here, plus the rest of the Alamo staff. I'd like you two to prepare a statement, maybe a page or so, if you're comfortable with that, because there will be a *huge* crowd here wanting to hear all about it."

Adam and Ashley smiled.

"We'd be honored," Adam said. They hugged Jane and headed back to the hotel.

Adam called Angela Amayo and Mark Martinez, who were both ecstatic. Martinez said he was going to head out at that moment to find Mr. Moreno and make sure he'd be available for Martinez to pick him up in his car the following morning for the drive to San Antonio.

"Mr. Moreno will be so thrilled," Martinez said. "I just wish we had a way to let Mr. Esparza know. I'll try in the coming months. I do have some contacts in Mexico. I promise I'll do all I can to get word to him."

"Thanks," Adam said. "We'll see you tomorrow at about 6:30 P.M. We're having the ceremony after the Alamo closes, just to keep things from getting out of control. And then, the day after tomorrow, the guns and the combined pieces of the note that we made on our computer will be on permanent display!"

"That's a very respectable thing you, your sister, and your parents did," Martinez said.

"And we learned a lot," Adam said. "We'll see you tomorrow. Have a safe trip."

Ashley then called Hannah. Angie answered the phone. She quickly filled Angie in and asked if she could bring Hannah.

"Sure; we wouldn't miss it for anything," Angie said. "Let me have you tell Hannah. Here you go."

"Hello?" Hannah said.

"Hi, Hannah, it's Ashley Arlington—we found the guns at the Alamo!" Ashley said.

"That's wonderful, dear!" Hannah said.

"We're having a ceremony tomorrow, after the Alamo closes," Ashley said.

"Angie is nodding her head," Hannah said, "so we'll be there. I'm so proud of you and Adam!"

"Thanks, Hannah; we'll see you tomorrow night then," Ashley said.

With only two days left in their vacation, the Arlingtons decided to take another stroll along the Riverwalk. Mrs. Arlington, who had gone downstairs to get soft drinks, returned with two envelopes. Inside were gift certificates for the bookstore across the street in the River-center Mall.

"Great!" Ashley said. "Thanks!"

"Thanks," Adam said. "I know what I'm getting—a couple more books on Texas history and the Alamo."

His parents smiled, having expected as much.

The Arlingtons headed out for a nice, long walk and had Mexican food for dinner at a riverside restaurant. Adam and Ashley each picked out books, which they mentioned would make the long drive home pass by a little faster.

When they got back to the hotel that night, their parents asked what they planned to do about the dedication.

"Your mother and I will head out for some ice cream, if you'd like an hour or two to put your heads together and come up with something," Mr. Arlington suggested.

Ashley and Adam agreed that was a good idea. They sat down after their parents grabbed light jackets and headed out of the hotel room.

"Ashley, you're the better speaker," Adam said. "I'd rather you gave the speech."

Ashley firmly shook her head from side to side. "No way," she told Adam. "I have some thoughts I'd love for you to include. But this is yours all the way, little bro."

They spent the next hour and a half writing a couple of pages of thoughts, first coming up with an outline of the things they wanted to mention and then filling in the text. Their parents were back just before 9 P.M. They had brought a few more souvenirs for Ashley and Adam.

"Let's talk," their mom said, holding her husband's hand as they both sat on the floor in front of Ashley and Adam, who were on the couch. "What did you two get out of this trip?"

Adam looked at Ashley. "I knew this was coming sooner or later," he said with a groan. "It's what-did-we-learn time again."

"Okay, okay," she said, grinning. "I'll go first. Well, the big thing for me was meeting people. I learned a long time ago that life is about people, not projects, even when we're doing something like this. I feel very fortunate we were able to meet Mr. Moreno, Mr. Martinez, and Mrs. Houston-Helgado, along with Jane and Angela. It was just an awesome, incredible journey. But Adam did a lot of the work."

"Good, Ashley," their mom said. "How about you, Adam?"

Adam looked at the holster.

"I don't think I've ever learned more on a vacation than I did on this one," he said. "I guess the thing that jumps into my mind first is that this wouldn't have ever started if I hadn't studied Spanish for so long. I wouldn't have even been able to get this from Mr. Esparza had I not spoken Spanish."

"That's a good point," Mr. Arlington said. "I was lost as you two were speaking back and forth. That kind of interest in other cultures and languages certainly served you well."

"Thanks," Adam said. "I also learned to keep the big picture in mind. Just like Hannah always focused on her piece of paper being related to San Jacinto, my mind was almost made up that our answers were at the Alamo. While those answers eventually were at the Alamo, we wouldn't ever have found what we were looking for if we hadn't taken the time to go to Goliad and San Jacinto. And that kind of leads to what else I learned. Whenever we go places, whether we have an adventure or not, I think we should learn as much about each state's history as possible. I understand so much better now the spirit of Texas, and its independent mind-set. I understand the love we should have for our Mexican and Tejano counterparts, because regardless of the side they were on, they had deep beliefs that we should respect. The Mexicans were backing the leader of their country. And the Tejanos helped shape Texas."

Adam paused, then said, "I guess that's about it."

"Well, that's outstanding," Mr. Arlington said. "The only criticism I think your mother and I could offer is that we might have been better served to wait to open the holster, otherwise it might not have been torn. On the other hand, had we involved too many people too soon by getting a professional to open it, we might have created a circus. So, all in all, you two kids did very well, and your mother and I are extremely proud of you."

Adam and Ashley thanked their parents, and each got hugs before they headed to bed.

"What a ride, Ash," Adam said.

"I don't know if I can sleep," Ashley said.

With that thought, they agreed they'd probably be up half the night because of all the excitement. But they had also been through a lot that day, and within fifteen minutes both were sound asleep.

But in their dreams, as their vacation wore down, they remembered the Alamo. They slept eight solid hours and didn't move until the next morning, when their parents came into the front of the suite to wake them.

History on Display

The next morning was again sunshiny and bright.

"We're headed out on bikes," Mrs. Arlington said, gently waking Ashley.

"Come on, buddy," Mr. Arlington said, rustling Adam. "We have all day until the dedication. We're going to bike for a few hours. We'll eat a good breakfast downstairs and then have a light lunch on the road. Your mother and I called and rented mountain bikes for the day."

While Adam and Ashley felt as if they couldn't wait until that evening's ceremony, they knew biking was a good, healthy way to dissipate their nervous energy and channel their excitement.

After a vigorous ride, they returned to the hotel at 3:30, got cleaned up and dressed nicely, then had a quick bite to eat at one of the sandwich shops in the mall before walking to the Alamo. Adam was carrying a big bag that he said included, "among other things," jackets and sweat-shirts.

When they got to the gate, Jane waved to them and had the guard unlock the gate to let them in, since the Alamo had been closed for more than half an hour.

Right away, they saw Mr. Moreno and Mr. Martinez.

"Hi!" Adam and Ashley said, rushing over to shake hands.

"Thank you, my friends," Mr. Moreno said. "This means more to me than you'll ever know."

Hannah came in too.

"We parked blocks away," Angie said. "And Hannah practically ran in here! I had to hurry to keep up with her."

Hannah hugged the entire Arlington family, who then introduced her to Mr. Moreno and Mark Martinez. Angela Amayo walked up, and more introductions were in order. Angela asked where she could find her old friend, Carolyn Carmen, and Jane pointed her toward the correct building.

"Can I, my friends, talk to Adam and Ashley alone for a moment?" Mr. Moreno asked the Arlingtons. They agreed, and he turned toward Hannah. "Ma'am, might you come too?"

"Certainly," Hannah said, wearing a puzzled look just as Ashley and Adam were. The four went about a dozen steps away. Mr. Moreno spoke for a moment, and then the others did too.

"What was that about?" Mrs. Arlington asked Ashley afterward.

"Can you wait?" Ashley asked. "I can tell you, but I think you'd enjoy it more if it were a surprise."

Jane assembled everyone in the area facing the well. Folding chairs had been lined up. Just a few steps from the well, on the stone walk, was a podium and microphone. Jane introduced herself and some of the dignitaries on hand, including some local politicians. TV crews caught the whole thing but were unobtrusive.

Next to the podium was a fiberglass container housing the guns mounted sharply on a piece of cast iron. The note that Adam had printed on his computer was alongside, along with one Jane had written up to explain the display once it was mounted inside the long barracks at the Alamo. Jane's note explained the paper Adam had put together and talked about how Bowie's legend had only grown. The six-shooters were a bit cleaner than they had been the day before, and both handles were facing out, so everyone who passed by would see the *J* and the *B* on them.

As Jane recounted what had been learned from the note, people were speechless. She retraced the Arlingtons' steps in the hunt, and then Jane had the Arlingtons stand up. She also asked Mr. Moreno to stand and say a few words. He stood but declined to say anything, other than waving and saying, "Thank you, to all my friends."

Jane also introduced Hannah Houston-Helgado, "a descendant of the great Sam Houston," and Hannah likewise declined to speak, other than to say, "I'm just glad to be here and meet such fine people."

Jane then asked Adam and Ashley to come to the front.

Adam grabbed Ashley's hand. "You bring Hannah, and I'll bring Mr. Moreno," he whispered, grabbing the bag he had brought.

"Adam needs a coat up there now?" Mr. Arlington asked his wife, laughing. She just shrugged her shoulders. She knew something was up but admittedly didn't know what it was.

Ashley went over to Hannah and walked her up, while Adam brought Mr. Moreno. The two flanked Adam and Ashley, who stood behind the podium.

"We'd like to start with a small surprise," Adam said. "I happened upon this mystery. Without Mr. Moreno and Mrs. Houston-Helgado, this hunt would have gone nowhere— as would have been the case had we not met fantastic folks like Jane Jermillo, Mark Martinez, and Angela Amayo. Myself, my sister, Mr. Moreno, and Mrs. Houston-Helgado talked on the phone last night, and again today. We'd like to add some things to this beautiful display case."

Mr. Moreno opened his vest as he had done before. Hannah pulled an envelope from her purse. As Mr. Moreno and Hannah held up their parts of the note, Adam fished into his bag and pulled out the plastic housing his part of the note.

"We want the Alamo to have the original note, in all its splendor and dilapidated glory," Adam said, drawing both applause and laughter.

Jane crossed her arms across her chest. "Thank you!" she said, putting her hands out flat and collecting all three pieces. She leaned into the microphone and said, "Now the display is complete because of the generosity of you, Mr. Moreno, you, Mrs. Houston-Helgado, and you, Adam and Ashley Arlington."

"Wait," Ashley said, stepping forward. "We make our donation in the name of Mr. Antonio Gregorio Esparza. Adam and I respectfully ask that our name not be on the donation sheet. Mr. Esparza and his family took good care of their part of the note for almost a century and a half."

Jane smiled at them and said she'd certainly respect their wishes. Adam stepped back up to the microphone.

"We'd also like to donate," Adam said, "again in the name of Mr. Antonio Gregorio Esparza, this to the Alamo."

Adam reached into the bag with both hands and carefully pulled out the holster.

"This belonged to James Bowie, and we have good reason to believe this holster might have at one time housed those two weapons, though we can't be sure," Adam said. The crowd roared with approval as Jane Jermillo came up and accepted the holster as a donation. Adam resumed his speech.

"I look at the paper we just handed to Ms. Jermillo," Adam said, "and I want everyone to realize that it came from Mexico. I think we should all pause and realize the sacrifice and loss of life that Mexico endured during these battles. On behalf of our Tejano friend, Mr. Moreno, we ask that everyone take a moment of silence to remember the commitment Tejanos made to the Texas cause and how important a place they occupy in Texas and American history. And finally, I want everyone to look at Hannah Houston-Helgado, the American in this trio. She is also, of course, a Texan. These three important groups—Mexicans, Tejanos, and Americans—all played, and still play, a part in what Texas was, is, and will become. We ask that everyone go an extra mile in the near future to meet someone from a different ethnic or geographical background than yourself. That's called progress—moving forward. And that, to me—an outsider—will symbolize the modern-day spirit of the Alamo, and the spirit of Texas, and of the United States."

Adam started to fold the paper. His speech complete, he and Ashley were almost overwhelmed by the standing ovation they received. They carefully walked Hannah and Mr. Moreno back to their seats, then sat down.

"Adam," Jane said as she prepared to finish the dedication, "I would like that copy of the speech you just recited. I'd like to display it with the six-shooters, the original parts of the letter, the combined copy you made on the computer, and the holster."

Adam stood.

"Come on, Ashley," Adam said, "you wrote a good part of this."

Ashley walked up to the front with Adam and gave the speech to Ms. Jermillo.

Then Jane officially dedicated the exhibit, pointing out every part of it, from the holster to the six-shooters to the original letter that started it all. With the ceremony complete, Adam and Ashley were able to meet a lot of the people in attendance and answer a lot of questions.

The next day, the family packed up the car. As they pulled out of San Antonio, they were on the interstate only fifteen minutes before they saw a sign indicating a flea market open at the next exit.

"No one," Mrs. Arlington said with a smile, looking toward the backseat, "says a word!"

Texas

*Fun
Fact
Files*

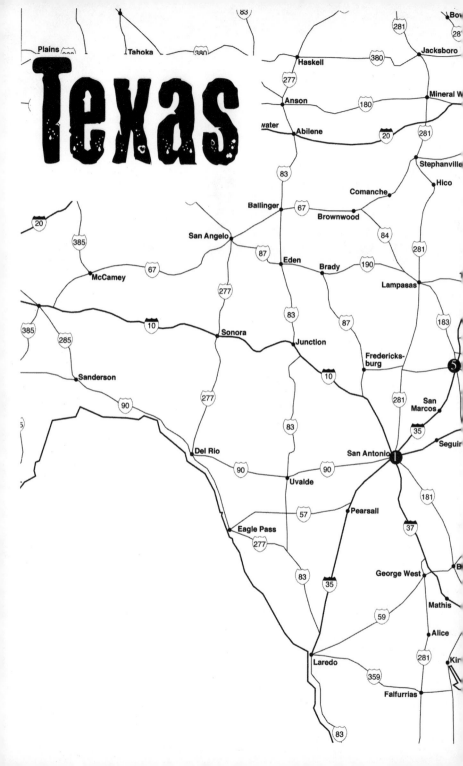

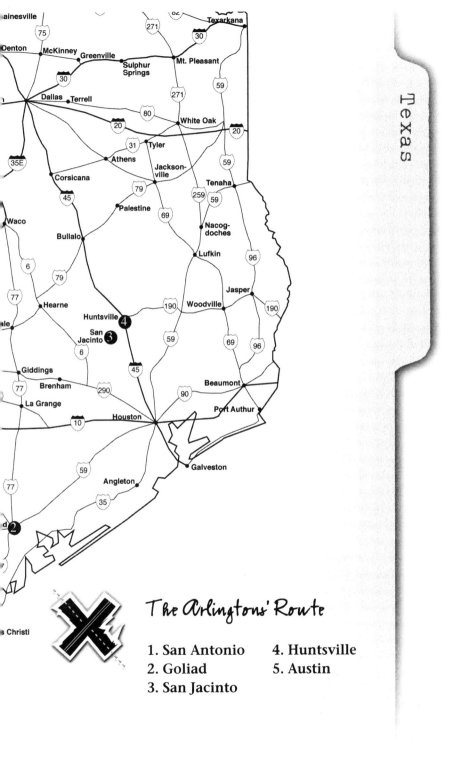

Texas

The Arlingtons' Route

1. San Antonio
2. Goliad
3. San Jacinto
4. Huntsville
5. Austin

Names and Symbols

Origin of Name:

Texas gets its name from the Hasinai Indian word tejas, which means friends or allies.

Nickname:

The Lone Star State

Motto:

"Friendship"

State Symbols:

flower: bluebonnet
tree: pecan
bird: mockingbird
mammal: Texas longhorn
gemstone: Texas blue topaz
fish: Guadalupe bass
song: "Texas, Our Texas"
dish: chili

Geography

Location:

Southwestern United States

Borders:

Gulf of Mexico (southeast)
Louisiana (east)
Arkansas (east and north)

Oklahoma (north and east)
New Mexico (west and north)
Mexico (southwest)

Area:

261,914 square miles (2d largest state—as large as
New England, New York, Pennsylvania, Ohio, and Illinois
combined)

Highest Elevation:

Guadalupe Peak (8,751 feet)

Nature

National Parks:

Big Bend National Park
Guadalupe Mountains National Park

National Forests:

Angelina National Forest
Davy Crockett National Forest
Sabine National Forest
Sam Houston National Forest

Weather

Texas has an extremely varied climate due to its size,
geographic position, and range of elevation. For
instance, rainfall in eastern Texas averages 50 inches

per year, while rainfall in western Texas averages less than 10 inches per year. In Brownsville, the southern-most city, no measurable snowfall has occurred in the twentieth century, but the northwestern corner has an average of 23 inches of snow per year. The highest recorded temperature in Texas is 120 degrees, while the lowest recorded temperature is 23 degrees below zero.

People and Cities

Population:

20.1 million (2000 census estimate)

Capital:

Austin

Ten Largest Cities:

Houston (1,749,001)
San Antonio (1,070,207)
Dallas (1,050,698)
El Paso (583,431)
Austin (557,532)
Fort Worth (478,307)
Arlington (288,227)
Corpus Christi (274,234)
Lubbock (194,522)
Garland (190,703)

Counties:

254

Major Industries

Agriculture:

Texas is one of the most important agricultural states in the country. It has more farms, farmland, sheep, and lambs than any other state, and it leads all the others in the raising of beef cattle, cotton, and cottonseed. Other principal crops are cotton lint, grains, sorghum, vegetables, citrus and other fruits, wheat, and rice. Texas also has an important fishing industry, with the principal catches being shrimp, oysters, and menhaden.

Mining:

Spindletop, in east Texas, was Texas's first oil gusher. Erupting in 1901, it began the state's oil boom. Texas ranks first in oil and natural gas production, as well as in oil-refining capacity. In fact, oil deposits have been found under more than two-thirds of the state's area. Texas also ranks first in the production of sulfur, crude gypsum, and magnesium.

Manufacturing:

The largest manufacturing employer in Texas is the production of electric and electronic equipment, followed by nonelectric machinery. Other manufactured goods include oil-field equipment, air conditioners, furniture, boats, household appliances, machinery, leather goods, and clothing.

History

Native Americans:

Between 1000 B.C. and the arrival of the Spanish in the 16th century, several Native American cultures existed in different parts of Texas. The Mound Builders settled in east Texas, built houses of mud plaster, and made beautiful pottery. The Basket Makers settled in the Texas Panhandle, lived in caves, and made baskets from the yucca plant. The first European explorers encountered the Caddo and the Hasinai, whom they found to be peaceful people. Other Native American tribes included the Wichita and the Apache. Late in the 18th century, the Comanche entered Texas and pushed the Apache southward. Today about 50,000 Native Americans live in Texas. There are three existing Indian reservations, but most Native Americans in Texas live outside the reservations.

Exploration and Settlement:

The Spanish were the first Europeans to explore Texas. In 1519 the first explorer, Alonzo Álvarez de Piñeda, mapped the coast of the Gulf of Mexico. In 1682 the Spanish established their first mission in Texas, near present-day El Paso. By the early 1800s, Spain's hold on Texas had weakened, and in 1821 Mexico won its independence from Spain and took over Texas. During this time many Anglo-Americans settled in Texas, which caused problems with the Mexicans. War broke out in 1835 and ended at the Battle of San Jacinto on April 21, 1836. Texas became an independent republic until it was annexed by the United States.

Territory:

The Republic of Texas existed for almost ten years before becoming a U.S. state.

Statehood:

It entered the union on December 29, 1845 (28th state).

Check It Out

For more information about the historical people and places in this book, check out the following books and web sites:

Texas

Web sites:

http://www.state.tx.us

http://www.lsjunction.com

http://tsha.utexas.edu/handbook/online

Goliad Massacre

Web sites:

http://lsjunction.com/events/goliad_m.htm

http://206.76.136.3/cfair/massacre.html

Battle of San Jacinto

Web sites:

http://www.lsjunction.com/events/jacinto.htm

http://www.tsha.utexas.edu/handbook/online/articles
/view/SS/qes.html

http://www.tpwd.state.tx.us/park/battlesh/battlesh.htm

Sam Houston

Book:

Fritz, Jean. Make Way for Sam Houston. New York:
Coward-McCann, 1986.

Web sites:

http://www.lsjunction.com/people/houston.htm

http://www.shsu.edu/~pin_www/HouSerL.html

http://www.tsl.state.tx.us/treasures/giants/houston-01.html

Battleship Texas

Web sites:

http://www.usstexasbb35.com

http://www.navsource.org/archives/01/35.htm

James Bowie

Web sites:

http://www.lsjunction.com/people/bowie.htm

http://www.tsha.utexas.edu/handbook/online/articles/view/BB/fbo45.html

---

Santa Anna

Web sites:

http://www.lsjunction.com/people/santann.htm

http://pbs.org/weta/thewest/people/s_z/santaanna.htm

The Alamo

Books:

Garland, Sherry, and Ronald Himler. Voices of the Alamo. New York: Scholastic Trade, 2000.

Sorrels, Roy. The Alamo in American History. Springfield, N.J.: Enslow Publishers, Inc., 1996.

Web sites:

http://www.drtl.org/webchro1.html

http:/www.thealamo.org

http://www.tuohy-alamo.com